Crooked Little Vein

Selected Graphic Novels by Warren Ellis

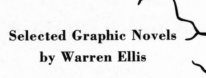

Desolation Jones (2006)

Fell (2007)

Global Frequency (2 volumes, 2002)

Lazarus Churchyard (1992, 2001)

Ministry of Space (2004)

Ocean (2005)

Orbiter (2003)

Scars (2003)

Transmetropolitan (10 volumes, 1997–2002)

Other Books by Warren Ellis

Come in Alone (comics industry/medium commentary)

Available Light (short fiction and photography)

CROOKED LITTLE VEIN

Warren Ellis

wm

WILLIAM MORROW
An Imprint of HarperCollins*Publishers*

This book is a work of fiction. The characters, incidents, and dialogue are drawn from the author's imagination and are not to be construed as real. Any resemblance to actual events or persons, living or dead, is entirely coincidental.

HarperCollins books may be purchased for educational, business, or sales promotional use. For information please write: Special Markets Department, HarperCollins Publishers, 10 East 53rd Street, New York, NY 10022.

FIRST EDITION

Designed by Kara Strubel

Library of Congress Cataloging-in-Publication Data has been applied for.

ISBN: 978-0-06-072393-4
ISBN-10: 0-06-072393-9

07 08 09 10 11 DT/RRD 10 9 8 7 6 5 4 3 2 1

To Niki and Lili, for continuing to put up with me,
and to the memory of my father

Crooked Little Vein

Chapter 1

I opened my eyes to see the rat taking a piss in my coffee mug. It was a huge brown bastard; had a body like a turd with legs and beady black eyes full of secret rat knowledge. Making a smug huffing sound, it threw itself from the table to the floor, and scuttled back into the hole in the wall where it had spent the last three months planning new ways to screw me around. I'd tried nailing wood over the gap in the wainscot, but it gnawed through it and spat the wet pieces into my shoes. After that, I spiked bait with warfarin, but the poison seemed to somehow cause it to evolve and become a super-rat. I nailed it across the eyes once with a lucky shot with the butt of my gun, but it got up again and shat in my telephone.

I dragged myself all the way awake, lurching forward in my office chair. The stink of rat urine steaming and festering in my mug stabbed me into unwelcome wake-fulness, but I'd rather have had coffee. I unstuck my backside from the sweaty leatherette of the chair, fought my way upright, and padded stiff-legged to the bath-room adjacent to my office. I knew that one of these days someone was going to burst into the office unannounced to find a naked private investigator taking a piss with the bathroom door open. There was a time where I cared about that sort of thing. Some time before I started living in my own office, I think.

My suit and shirt were piled on the plastic chair I use for clients. I stole it from a twenty-four-hour diner off Union Square, back in my professional drinking days. I picked up the shirt and sniffed it experimentally. It seemed to me that it'd last another day before it had to be washed, although there was a nagging thought at the back of my mind that maybe it actually reeked and my sense of smell was shot. I held up the sleeve and exam-ined the armpit. Slightly yellowish. But then, so was everything else in the office. No one would see it with the jacket on, anyway.

I rifled the jacket for cigarettes, harvested one, and went back to my chair. I swabbed some of the nicotine scum off the window behind the chair with the edge of my hand and peered down at my little piece of Manhattan street.

It occurs to me now that if I hadn't seen the man in black on the far side of the street at that exact second, I would probably still be brushing my teeth with bleach.

But I did. The absolute stereotypical man in black, with the shades and the earpiece and the stone face.

And another, down the street.

I leaned over. A third was outside the door to my building.

And they were all looking up at my window.

"Well, you always knew this could happen," I told myself, because there was no one else around to give me a hard time.

A black car pulled up under my window. My office is five stories up. Takes me six minutes, in my shattered condition, to ascend the stairs to my door. Call it three for someone in basic human condition. I had exactly that long to get dressed and think of something clever.

But I wasted another terrified thirty seconds watching the car disgorge three more people who headed directly into my building.

I almost put my foot through the crotch of my pants in my hurry to dress. No idea who they were or what they wanted but a very basic sense of self-preservation said, Mike, you need to be running in the general direction of Away now. Three buttons of the shirt done up, fuck the other three, stuff the tie in the pocket, pull on the jacket, practically break your fucking ankle getting the shoes on. Half-run, half-fall for the door. Left the gun back in my desk. I needed the gun. I thought I needed the gun. Ran back into the office, sat down on my sticky chair, pulled at the lower left drawer where the gun sits, and the door opened. The outer door to my office.

Two men in black swept through the small reception room and in, looking down extended arms and two-handed grips full of large gun at me. They bobbed and pivoted around my office like gangster marionettes. One of them broke the effect by bringing his right hand up and talking into his sleeve. "All clear. Needle can enter at will."

A bony man with skin like leather in a suit that seemed to not quite fit him walked quickly into my office. The men in black deferred to him and swept out, closing the door behind them. I was suddenly alone with the bony man, whose face was vaguely familiar to me.

The bony man sat in my client's chair, eyed me sourly. "Do you know who I am, son?"

The voice fitted to the deathly presence. I'd seen him on the news, but this was not a man made for television. "You work for the president, don't you?"

He nodded once. "I'm the chief of staff to the office of the President of the United States. And you are Michael McGill. Can I call you Mike?"

"No, I'm . . ." Reflex. Swallowed, changed tracks. "Mike is fine." I slumped in my chair. "I really need to be more awake than this." The square inch of my brain that was working properly blitzed through possibilities. It's a gag. No, that's the guy. Why is the chief of staff alone in a room with a man whom they must know has a gun in the drawer? No, no, that's the cart before the horse: why is he here looking at me like that? With those eyes, so pale they're almost white-on-white? Jesus, he's a creepy old fart in real life . . .

"You're looking at me strangely, son."

I smiled, shook my head. "It's just what TV does to us. You say 'chief of staff' and I expect John Spencer from *The West Wing*, you know? I don't suppose you're a genial man of Chicago with a drink problem, right?"

"Hell, no. I take heroin, son."

"Okay."

"I have a stressful job. This is how I like to relax. I like to go to a small hotel and take heroin. Just lay on the bed and feel my bowels slowly unclench."

He leaned back and sighed with relish, as if he were sinking into a warm bath.

"I like to lay on the bed, naked, with my guts oozing onto the sheets, nodding out and watching the Fashion Channel. All those skeletal smacked-out girls. The faces of angels and the bodies of Ethiopians. I find that

7

sexy, son. It's not like I have an easy job, and I feel I should be cut some slack in this area. Heroin angels, strutting around for me. With Enya playing. They play a lot of Enya on the Fashion Channel. Great regiments of heroin angels lined up in endless long dressing rooms elegantly banging smack between their delicate toes to the sound track of British TV shows about Celtic people. You should try it. It's a poetic thing, you know?"

His eyes closed, a beatific grin spreading across his weathered face like an old wound opening.

"In that moment, son, I am as beautiful as they, and you are to ignore the rabbit droppings steaming on my bed: interior chocolates placed on the pillow by the solicitous maids of my bowel. Sometimes I get up and dance, scattering the gifts of my intestines across the Edwardian carpet, ignoring the shrieking of the house-keepers and the priests they call in. 'Phone the White House,' I sing to them. 'I control the nuclear bombs.' All of which is to say: I am a functioning heroin addict and also the most powerful man in the world, and you should pay attention now."

He hadn't opened his eyes. The gun was in the desk drawer. Five, six inches away from my hand. It was tempting. I hadn't decided which of us to use it on, though.

"Oh, I am. Insofar as I'm wondering what the hell you're doing here."

"I'm here because you're a shit magnet, son."

It was one of those unusual moments where I couldn't think of a swearword bad enough.

"The world just kind of happens to you, son. The worst things we could possibly imagine just up out of nowhere and piss on your shoes, don't they? It's a special talent. It gets you work as an investigator, and in certain circles you are renowned for plucking diamonds from that skyscraper of blood-flecked turds that is the American cultural underworld."

"Don't you have a divorce case for me? A lost dog? Missing doorkeys?" I don't think there was a sob in that last bit.

"Those are for ordinary people, son. You are special."

"What I am is unlucky," I snarled. "You know I got an adultery case last year? You know what the husband turned out to be doing at night? He had formed a sex cult that broke into an ostrich farm at midnight three times a week. You know what it's like, finding eight middle-aged guys having tantric sex with ostriches?"

The chief of staff made a sympathetic noise he'd probably learned off a talk show. "I'm not sure I can even imagine how to do that."

"I had that image in my head for two months. I couldn't have sex. My girlfriend came to bed one night in a feather boa and I started crying. She left me for a woman named Bob who designs strap-ons shaped like dolphin penises."

"That's very sad, son."

"Bob had a hair transplant procedure on her nipples. They email me photographs."

"I'm sorry for your pain. But this only illustrates how you are the right man for this job."

"I'm not the right man for any job. You want to call me a shit magnet, fine, I'm a shit magnet. But what I am is the unluckiest bastard you ever met. I have to take this work because it's all I can do, but please, I don't look for this stuff."

"No. It finds you. Which is why you are perfect for this job. We have something we need you to find, and we have exhausted all our orthodox operations. Somewhere out there is a book we need."

"Lost and found?" I said, hopeful.

And right there is where I needed a time machine, so I could go back and shoot myself.

"Lost and found. Lost in the 1950s, in fact. Nixon traded it for the favors of a Chinese woman living on a houseboat in San Francisco Bay. It's moved from person to person ever since. Now we need it back in the White House."

A cold fifty-year-old trail. That was some real detective work right there. This had a weird appeal to me. It seemed like what the job should be about. As opposed to waving a flashlight over a fat bank manager hunched over an ostrich full of Rohypnol.

"I'll need to know what the book is."

"Yeah. This is the tricky part. Technically, this is high codeword stuff. I've had your name signed to a document that allows you to know the following, on pain of death if the information exits your train of investigation."

"Excuse me?"

"You talk about this, the Office of Homeland Security turns you into pink mist. There will be Shock and Awe, do you understand?"

That took me a minute. Getting my head around their having apparently forged my signature on a White House document. In my experience, people in positions of overwhelming power don't lie. They don't have to. I shifted in my chair, sketched a small smile, and tried to speak, but all that came out was a choking sound. The chief of staff seemed to take this as a yes. Or simply decided that I was scared enough.

"We need you to find the other Constitution of the United States."

I carefully kept my face neutral and composed. You know, professional.

"This is a secret document privately authored by several of the Founders. It details the real intent of their design of American society, and twenty-three Invisible Amendments to be read and adhered to only by the presidents, vice-presidents, and chiefs of staff.

"It is a small, handwritten volume reputedly bound in the skin of the extraterrestrial entity that plagued Benjamin Franklin's ass over six nights in Paris during his European travels. Benjamin Franklin wasn't some nancy-boy novelist who wrote sensitive books about aliens sticking things up his rectum, you know. On the seventh night he got right up and killed the little bastard with one punch."

I didn't want to move. It felt like I was trapped in a room opposite a mad weasel with paintstripper daubed on its nipples. One false motion and it'd stop ripping itself to shreds right in front of you and go straight to chewing your head into a stump.

He just wouldn't stop talking. It was horrible.

"The book binding is weighted with meteor fragments. The design is such that the sound of the book being opened onto a table has infrasonic content, too low for human hearing. The book briefly vibrates at eighteen hertz, which is the resonant frequency of the human eyeball."

He lurched forward, fixing me with a fanatic gaze. "Do you *understand*, son? Do you *see*? *It's a book that forces you to read it.* It prepares your eye for *input*."

I met his eyes and mirrored his pose to try and calm him a little, make him know I was on his side. I was abstractly aware of my hand shaking and I needed to bring this back down to earth any way I could.

"Okay, sir. You've lost a valuable private historical document—"

"It's more than that. I want you to *comprehend*. We need this book. How can I put it? Do you like living in America, Mike?"

"Sure, I guess. Never lived anywhere else."

"You don't think America's changed? That maybe it was once a better place to live?"

"Well. I've seen America change, certainly. Whether it was better or not, I don't know. I don't recall the eighties as being much fun, and the nineties were just kind of there, you know?"

"Yeah. You're young. You don't see it. When I was young, Mike, this country was pure, and righteous. Secure in the knowledge that we had fought pure evil and won. Furthermore, every able-bodied man in America had been trained in killing people with dangerous firearms. I could walk home from school without fear of being set upon by testicular saline infusion fetishists. Those people, by the way, are not to be trusted. You need to remember that.

"The country has changed, Mike, year by year, day by

13

day. Look at what's on television now. Look at the magazines and newspapers. Look at what people put on the Internet. These aren't hidden perversions, Mike. This isn't like Dr. Sawyer and the collection of black men's tongues he kept in that weird little house on the outskirts of town when I was twelve. This is the mainstream now, Mike. This is how life in America *is*. Moment by moment, our country has grown sicker. Our borders, Mike, have come to encompass the nine circles of Hell."

He suddenly seemed very small and lonely.

"Since the book was lost, Mike. It's all happened since the book was lost. We need the book back. We need to study it and apply it and make America beautiful again."

I took a deep breath. The next thirty seconds were either going to save me or kill me, I figured. "You realize I couldn't care less about that, right?"

I wanted him to, I dunno, react like he was shot, or call his creatures in to shoot me, or anything that was going to get me off this hook I'd been spiked on.

He wasn't supposed to smile like that.

"We know," the chief of staff said happily. "This clinched your selection. You see, Mike, what we really need is a human shit-tick, swimming through the toilet bowl of America. We don't need someone who's going to crawl to the edge and demand a blue-block and a flush.

14

We need someone content to paddle through the droppings. Someone who doesn't care about anything but doing their job. That you are some kind of moral mutant who bears no love for the country that gives them life is, amazingly, what suits you best to the task at hand."

My face sank down into my hands. "Oh, good," I mumbled. Or "Oh, God." One of the two.

"Smile, son. In five minutes' time, there will be half a million dollars in your bank account, available for immediate withdrawal. Yours, nonrecoupable. Tax-free, too."

I could feel my face involuntarily twisting into a wonky grin. My mom had a regular saying: "I don't know whether to laugh or cry." It usually came out when the police came to tell us Dad had turned up naked someplace again. Sometimes it made me laugh, sometimes it made me cry, but I never felt torn between the two, and sometimes I thought Mom was crazier than Dad for saying it. But this was it. I didn't know whether to laugh out loud (because it was true, or because he was full of shit) or burst into tears right there and then (because he'd really done it, or because he was lying). I didn't know what to believe and I didn't know how to react. I wasn't scared so much anymore. I just resented the old bastard for making me feel like that.

He reached into his jacket pocket, withdrew a flat black plastic thing that he handed over to me. I took it, suspiciously, and gingerly explored the seam my fingertips found on the long side. A catch snicked, and it unfolded into a clamshell-style handheld computer.

"That's yours," the chief of staff said as it hissed into life in my hand, its long screen flaring clean white. "It contains all the leads we currently have, and is fitted for wireless Internet access. It goes into a secure system at Treasury, which pushes continuing updates into your machine."

"You're just sending me into the wild with half a mil and this?"

"Oh, I will come to see you from time to time, when I have new information. Or perhaps just to see how you're doing and where you are. Consider me Virgil to your Dante." This notion amused him no end. His laugh was a dry, raspy, high thing, the sound of skeletons giggling.

He stood up, arranging his baggy suit on his pointy frame. "Smile, son. You are engaged in a great work. Everything is different now. You have the most glorious of goals. You are going to help us save America."

His eyes glittered like new coins.

"From itself."

I realized the chief of staff was preparing to leave. I surged out of the chair. "Hold on. I don't accept commissions just like this. I need, I need, some way to contact you, a longer briefing, something . . ."

"It's all in the machine. In a few minutes, you'll have all the expense money you could want. You contact me through a secure email system, I contact you when I deem it appropriate. Let's be men here: you know I'll be watching."

He extended one long tough hand. "Good hunting, Mr. McGill." I shook it. I could feel the little bones of his hand moving under my grip, like he was nothing but thin leather and sticks.

He did that curt nod again, spun on his heel, and left.

I looked at the closed door for about a minute. Then sat down again, heavily, and looked out the window. The men in black were melting away. I watched the street a while longer. The chief of staff and his security team came out of my building. He stopped. Looked up at me. His face split open in an awful grin. His team gathered him into his car, and they were off, gone, disappeared, like they were never there.

Except I had a brand-new handheld computer on my desk.

I had a thought. Opened the thing up again, tapped the icon for Internet access with my fingernail, and put a Web site address into it with the QWERTY thumbpad. My bank has an online service that I use in preference to the bank tellers laughing at my balance in front of me. I thumbed in the security number and waited.

I had half a million dollars in my bank account. In fact, I had five hundred thousand and three dollars and forty-one cents. The three forty-one was the sum total of my worldly wealth when I woke up that day.

The handheld thumped down on the desk, next to the cooling mug of rat piss. That was it. I had the biggest single-job expense account I'd ever seen, and the most insane job I'd ever heard of. Finding a book that had been lost for fifty years. If it had ever existed. A secret Constitution of the United States. Invisible Amendments. Hell, I couldn't tell you how many *visible* Amendments there were.

I had half a million dollars. For a complete wild-goose chase. Half a million dollars that were mine and never to be spent on anything remotely useful.

Chapter 2

I sat there for at least half an hour, just thinking. Trying to think, anyway. Sort of a fugue state, where lots of words were flying around my head without assembling into sentences. The walls started closing in. Shifting in my chair, I found that my joints were locking up and my muscles were bunching into hard knots of stress. I fought my way into my jacket, feeling like a stick insect trying to put on a life vest, and went out for a walk.

There was a girl with blue hair sitting cross-legged on the corner of the street. Her hair fell down her back in thick, fuzzy dreadlocks, like someone had nailed a dozen baby aliens to her head. She was dressed in what I assumed to be an artful arrangement of fabric swatches intended to resemble rags, rather than actual shambling homeless/nutcase out-and-out rags. Tartan, paisley, plaid, things that looked like they belonged as wallpaper in a kid's room, things that looked like they'd been ripped off clowns at knifepoint. She had her back to me, and, as I approached, I expected to see a hat in front of her, or a little cardboard sign with the hand-scrawled message NEED MONEY FOR FOOD/DRUGS/CLOWN-STABBING. As I walked around her, I saw that she was just sitting there, eyes closed, hands on her knees, perfectly still and calm.

She had . . . well, I thought it was Sharpie or makeup around her eye, at first. A wobbly circle, with stitch marks crossing it, drawn like the sort of roundish patch you'd see sewn into teddy bears or old denim jeans. She sort of came to as I walked around her, smiled as if she'd just woken up, and rubbed her face. The marking didn't smear. It was tattooed on.

She rubbed her eyes, and then looked up at me, giving me the gentlest smile. "Hello," she said softly.

"Are you okay?"

"I'm fine. Why wouldn't I be?"

"You're sitting asleep on the corner of the street."

"I wasn't asleep. I was listening."

"To what?"

She nodded at the street, still with that serene smile. "The traffic. Sit with me." She patted the sidewalk next to her. Calculating that, after this, the day just couldn't get any weirder, I said the hell with it and sat down next to her.

She nodded toward the street. "The traffic. I'm listening to the traffic."

"What's so interesting about the sound of cars? Is this one of those art things I never get?"

She laughed, and it was a soft low laugh, like the flow of water in a brook. There was no tension in the girl at all. I couldn't imagine anything affecting that pool of relaxation around her. Just sitting there, I felt the knots in my back slowly sliding apart.

"No. Well, not really. I'm listening for the future."

"The future."

"Do you know anything about the Native Americans?"

"Only the usual stuff about poisoning them with infected blankets. I always wondered why we don't give little blankets to each other at Thanksgiving."

There was almost a frown there. "That's just nasty."

"I'm sorry," I said. It came out of me without really thinking. I suddenly didn't want to spoil her and her zone of no-tension.

"The Native American shamans," she said, "listened for the future in the sound of horses. They divined it, from the patterns of hoofbeats. They would sit like this, and just listen. In those days, horses were the sound of their world, the true sound of motion, and they believed that their movement through time let in leakages of the future. Presentiments of what will be."

"I don't see any horses."

"Then you're not looking." She smiled, indulgent. "This is the sound of our world in motion, right here. Cars. The strike of hooves became the point where the rubber meets the road. Now, I'm a new American. My family came over on the boat from Spain only a hundred years ago. But that doesn't mean I can't learn from the people who were here before. In fact, I think it means I 'must' learn from them, if I'm going to stay here and look after this land properly. If only to make up for your smallpox-infected blankets, right? So here I sit. A New American shaman, divining the future from the sound of cars."

As the strangeness of my days go, this was really kind of benign in its insanity. And I was enjoying the peace of her. So I drew my knees up and around until I was cross-legged like her, and we sat together like Zen hoboes on the corner of the street.

"What do you hear?" I asked.

She inclined her head slightly, toward the constant blur of metal accelerating past us. Just listening. It took a minute before she gave a little laugh.

"What?" I said.

"I hate the way this sounds. It makes me sound like a carny fortune-teller."

"Go on."

"You're going on a long journey, Mike."

"Oh, God. Tell me there's no tall dark stranger."

She giggled. "I think you're the tall dark stranger. But, no, you're going on a long journey. Sounds like you're going to cross the country before you're done. And yourself. It's going to be strange for you. But that's not a bad thing. Traveling is good."

"You travel a lot?"

"I do nothing but travel," she said, glancing at me. "Look at my face. I don't fit in anywhere. I can't get a job, buy a house, any of the things we're supposed to want to do. When I got the tattoo, I knew I was drawing a crooked line between myself and society. But that's okay. It stops me from giving up on myself. It stops me from settling for something ordinary. You shouldn't want ordinary things, either. You're unusual. I know you can't hear the future, but it comes to you, anyway, doesn't it?"

"I don't know that I'd call it the future."

"That's because you can't hear it."

"Back up a second," I said, feeling like I'd missed a step. "I just thought of something."

"What?"

"I didn't tell you my name."

"No." She smiled. "You didn't."

"I should really get moving," I said, standing up, suddenly very cold.

She beamed up at me. "Yes, you should. You just came into quite a lot of money. You should spend a little on yourself before you have to spend it on necessities. You don't need to start your journey just yet. Enjoy yourself a little bit."

"I just thought of an old song," I said.

"Which one?"

"'Enjoy yourself. It's later than you think.'"

"That's right," she said, eyes drawn back to the traffic. "It's always later than you think. I won't be here tomorrow. And neither will you. Go have a drink."

Chapter 3

An hour later, I walked into some freak bar on Bleecker Street and yelled, "I'm buying a hundred drinks—for *me*!"

Oh, they beat the shit out of me.

Chapter 4

By Sunday, I'd moved into the Z Hotel, where the door-
men dress like ninjas and stab passing poor people in
the neckbits with wooden swords.

I spent the day reading the handheld, in between horrible abuse of room service and watching all the Filth-O-
Vision pay-TV porno I could handle. It turned out that
regular vanilla sex hadn't been changed while I'd been
away in the prison of chastity forced upon me by the
world, but apparently all men and women everywhere
now like anal sex, and no one uses a rubber to prevent
pregnancy when there is the opportunity to ejaculate up
a woman's nostril.

There was actually a porno documentary pasted
between the hump flicks as "bonus programming." A
scrawny girl with pretty eyes and teeth like a ninety-

year-old chainsmoker cackled to the camera that, while tampering with her female coperformer, her "entire fuckin' arm went right up there! It was awesome!" Sitting there naked but for a light crusting of popcorn crumbs, I scratched my belly and considered for a few moments the erotic voltage of someone's forearm suddenly appearing in your abdomen. I just couldn't see it.

A thin man in a jacket someone had plainly advised him to buy as a sick joke sat in front of the camera next, attending carefully to his 1983 flicked hair with a sensitive palm. He was one of those disturbing people who only appear to have a chin from certain angles. When he inclined his head, his chin became a tiny couch-like thing sitting an inch above his collarbone. He was introduced as America's premier male adult performer. It was explained that he was a triple threat as producer, writer, and trained cock with body attached. Despite plainly being convinced that he was also America's greatest comedy genius ("I have *two* funny voices. That's one more than most people. John Cleese only has one funny voice."), he wasn't entirely stupid. He had a Kim Jong Il–like moment where he seemed to claim that he'd invented anal sex, but he said something interesting after that.

"Anal sex was edgy. It wasn't a mainstream thing. But time was, cum shots were edgy. And there was a response to cum shots, and then every porno had cum shots, and now there's bukkake. Same with anal sex. Big shock when it was first shown, and now anal sex is in every movie. The audience takes that on and then says, What's next? What's new? So all this stuff, that was hidden away for years, is mainstream now. You know what else? There was a movie in England last year, an arty movie, based on a literary kind of novel. And it has blowjobs. The actress—and this was straight actors and actresses, not adult performers—had to suck the actor off on camera. Porno's already crossed over, man. We're mainstream American shit now. If people out there want to worry about something, tell them to worry about what comes next. Worry about what comes after us."

I had no idea what bukkake was, and absolutely no interest in finding out. But the rest of it resonated with what the chief of staff had said to me the day before. Things people tried to not even conceive of in the 1950s were matter-of-fact daily life in the 00s.

Is it the Oh-Ohs, I wondered? Or the Zero-Zeros? More beer was required to puzzle this one out.

The room service people pleaded with me not to answer the door dressed entirely in popcorn again.

I put the phone down, picked up the handheld again, and sank into the luxurious sofa with it.

If the documents filling the handheld were to be believed, they'd spent the last two years using every paranoia-inducing spook operation you've ever heard of in tracking the book down. FBI, CIA, NSA, even ISA, which I knew were the president's own spooks, formed by Carter in the seventies. Lots of rumors, third-party reports, hearsay and bullshit, and a litany of hotspots missed by months or years.

The book didn't seem to stay in anyone's hands for long. It appeared to be considered an asset to be traded. The mysterious Chinese woman from San Francisco started the game by trading it to a rogue private hospital in Texas in return for a multiple trepanation operation. She had a circle of small holes drilled in her head, just below the hairline, that supposedly allowed her to transmit hypnotic mental radio. She died in Guatemala in 1985, attended by eighty-eight Fortune 500 figures, all of whom had enjoyed extended sexual knowledge of her.

The book stayed in Texas for six months, before being traded to an unknown figure in NASA in return for one of their experimental neural implant transceivers. A notation insisted that the patent actually exists, and was lodged by NASA—a two-way radio smaller than a dime and designed to be placed directly into the brain. Spaceflight is all about reducing the weight of whatever you're trying to fire into orbit, and two ounces in the brain has to be better than ten pounds of radio in the cockpit.

Unless you're the guy having a jagged circle of steel built with lowest-bidder components wedged into your living brain, I guess.

Additional notation explained that a secret NASA memo released on the Internet in 1996 revealed that the TV show *The Six Million Dollar Man* was actually a CIA blind created specifically to cover a possible breach of security over astronauts with extensive bioelectronic modification escaping the system and going public.

The documentation went on in this style for some considerable volume. I started skipping, decided to just see where in the stack of files I'd land.

I landed on New York City, two years ago.

A private group called NULL (notation: "colossal perverts") held the book for a month. Traded as a hush payment by a financially embarrassed mayoral candidate in return for silence over unnamed sexual proclivities, given to a major city landlord in return for lifetime free rent on a small building in SoHo.

It was Sunday night. I thought I'd go and take a look at the building, case it for a proper visit Monday or Tuesday, after I'd bought some new clothes.

I blasted the crumbs off my skin in the shower, and got hot water in my beer.

The sun was down by the time I got down to the lobby, full of people who worked for rich people. The rich people stay somewhere else. Their people stay at the Z on the expense account. People, talking about being people with people. People shoptalk. The people community. Magazine-beautiful, but almost pathologically uncharismatic. A swarm of pretty drones. Several of them looked me up and down. I was just unshaven, disheveled, stinking, and confused-looking enough to be Somebody. They weighed my wallet with X-ray vision. Perhaps I needed people.

I navigated past the swarm as best I could. Some of them floated in my direction while appearing to be continuing their conversations. I rearranged my jacket, allowing them to see my gun. Six backed off, but three got erections.

The ninja doorcrew on the sidewalk were scratching their nuts and talking about going to Mulberry Street for some clams. "Ywannacab?" One of them launched himself out into the middle of Lexington Avenue, howled like Bruce Lee being enthusiastically taken from behind, and waved his special ninja sword a lot. A yellow cab swerved over from the far lane and had a good crack at harvesting the door ninja off his left fender.

I didn't have the heart to tell him I didn't actually want a cab.

So I let the cabbie take me back to the Village, getting into the tangle of it, headed for the backstreet address in the handheld. The cabbie was white and extremely proud of it. He was of the opinion that he was the Last White Cabbie in New York City, in fact, because all of the others were fucken monkeys who got off the fucken boat and the fucken city said welcome to fucken America oh and have a fucken taxi driver medallion while you're fucken at it you fucken monkey you.

The property that had been held for this group was a narrow building with back-alley access. There was a handpainted wooden sign propped up by the front door. Whoever made it had gotten all their knowledge of the written word through cave painting. A legless guy on the corner, perched on an ancient diarrhea-stained skateboard, watched me as I kind of bent to the side and squinted at the sign, struggling to translate it. The word NULL was clear. The other major term seemed to be MHP BUKKAKE. Bukkake, whatever it was, appeared to be hip among the young folk of today.

So, like an idiot, I went in.

The hall was lit by a single lamp with a green shade, turning everything the color of snot. A large man who appeared not to know he was bald sat at a chair and table boosted from a school, asscheeks overflowing the seat's weathered plastic. He clanked a tin box full of coins at me. "Two bucks," he croaked. His neck inflated like a frog's when he spoke.

"For what?"

"It's movie night, man."

"Shit, I forgot," I covered. I gave him ten bucks. "For the cause, dude."

"Cool." He took the ten bucks, made to put it in the box, and then pocketed it when he thought I wasn't looking.

It was a walk-up—the only way to go was upstairs. Tinny noise clattered down the stairs. I headed up.

It was dark and big. Most of the walls on that floor had been knocked out, turning it into a makeshift auditorium. The seating was several rows of interlocking plastic chairs. Must've been fifty people in there, halflit by the glow of the movie being projected onto one long wall, plastered smooth and painted white. I took the first free seat close to the staircase I could find. The movie glow let me read the white plastic ink on the T-shirt of the big guy next to me: NO, I WON'T FIX YOUR FUCKING COMPUTER.

It was a Godzilla movie, one of the old Japanese ones. Some poor mad bastard strapped into a rubber lizard suit and paid ramen money to stomp on a balsa model of Tokyo.

There was a clumsy cut, and then another pretend lizard-monster clumped across a bonsai Tokyo. The picture quality was different. It was cut in from another movie. Cut back to Godzilla; but in slow motion, with a rose filter over the image, and what sounded like Justin Timberlake mixed in over the top.

There was a perceptible shift in the audience. I heard the guy next to me hold his breath.

More rubber lizards appeared, cut in from what could have been half a dozen movies. Then a long, loving tracking shot of Godzilla, from his lizard toes up to his bulging eyes. The music swelled. Another cut; white doves flying. And then a snatch of homemade film, someone in a Godzilla mask, going "Grrrrh" in a way that sounded distinctly American.

Someone across the room said. "Yeahhh," and I looked across. My eyes were adjusting to the dark now. Mostly men, in T-shirts and shorts. A few women, dressed the same way, obviously there with boyfriends. The only woman who looked to be there alone was a skinny girl on the far side, with dyed-black hair, a dyed-black wifebeater, and what looked like full-sleeve tattoos. I panned back, and for the first time got a good look at the guy next to me.

He was wearing a large green foam glove molded to resemble a lizard paw on his right hand. And his right hand was placed very determinedly on his crotch.

On the screen, Godzilla was wrestling with another lizard monster. Gasps from a porno flick were laid over the top.

Someone groaned in the dark. I looked over to see a woman rubbing her boyfriend's lap with a lizard-paw glove.

"This isn't fair," I hissed, hating the world for insisting on always fucking doing this to me.

The guy next to me turned around. Sweat glittered on his forehead. "Dude," he whispered, "you didn't get a glove?"

"No, it's . . . no one's told me what MHP means, that's all." I wasn't going to admit I didn't know what bukkake was, since it was so obviously a badge of the cool.

He smiled in the dark, showing me teeth that would've made Shane MacGowan puke. "You didn't know we got a word now? Damn, you've been away, dude. Macroherpetophile. Herpetophile, for people who, you know, like lizards. *Like* lizards. And macro for like, big, large scale. So, like, people who . . ."

People who want to fuck Godzilla.

The sound track erupted with a roar mixed with an aggressive orgasm, and his beady eyes snapped back to the screen. Godzilla had his teeth in the neck of another reptile. The audience was heaving now, a subsonic rumble of deep gasping, fifty people radiating wet heat into the auditorium.

The tattooed girl took out a little handheld, backlit, and was scratching notes into its handwriting-recognition system with a stylus.

Godzilla had a lizardy thing down in the dirt, grappling wildly. The guy next to me groaned, "Yeah, take it, you bitch . . ."

Donna Summer's "I Feel Love" entered the sound track.

The guy next to me began frantically scrubbing his crotch with the glove. I decided to keep my eyes on the screen. It was obvious to me by this point that I was never ever going to have sex again, and I just needed to get through this until the lights came up and I could find someone to question.

As Donna Summer started into the last lap toward her fake orgasm, the image began to cut back to the new footage of the person in the mask. By this point, everyone else in the room was getting there, too. Aside from a guy in the back, who was being berated by his girlfriend by letting fly too soon. He was getting pissed and growling "You *knew* not to make me think about the scales."

There was a flash of white on the screen. It took me a

second to realize that, in the new footage, someone had ejaculated on the mask. And then again. Donna Summer let rip. The mask was battered with a dozen ejaculations. And the room erupted. I covered my face as the guy next to me practically bucked himself off his seat.

"Bukkake," said a voice in my ear. "Multiple ejaculations onto the face. It's the new thing." It was the tattooed girl, crouched behind my chair. "This is the only genuine and authentic Godzilla Bukkake night in America."

I twisted around to look at her, as the rest of the audience squeezed out their last drops into green foam paws. Her eyes were green, too. "You're not a dinosaur fetishist," she said, studying my face. "Why are you here?"

"I'll tell you if you tell me more about this place."

"Deal. You look a bit pale, and I don't think you want to see the clean-up session."

The door guy entered the room, carrying cages of thirsty-looking monitor lizards, long tongues flicking.

I ran so fast there was a vapor trail.

Chapter 5

Outside, I scrabbled for my cigarettes, still vaguely angry at the world. The tattooed girl stole one off me and lit up with a plastic lighter in the shape of a baby alien. We leaned back against the nearest wall and exhaled up into the night air, little prayers that our passive smoke would kill someone we didn't like.

"I'm Mike."

"Trix."

"Hello, Trix."

"What were you doing there, Mike? There's no way you're MHP."

"I'm a private investigator. This place was an old lead I wanted to follow up on. But the usual happened."

"What's the usual?"

"Doesn't matter. You stood out in there, too, you know."

"Yeah, I guess. I'm writing a thesis."

"On what?"

"Extremes of self-inflicted human experience. It's not everyone who subjects themselves to Godzilla bukkake, after all."

She had a dirty laugh. Green eyes studied me from picture frames of intricate eyeliner and shadow. I was abstractly aware of wanting her to like me.

"Got anything about tantric ostrich date-rape in your thesis?"

Her eyes sparkled in the dark.

"Come on. I'll buy you a coffee. You can tell me about the Godzilla fetishists and I'll tell you the story."

"Buy me vodka and you've got a deal."

We took a cab to the Shark Bar, a block down from CBGB, where they skinned anyone who complained about cigarette smoke. The barman wore the scalp of a Straight Edge punk boy from San Jose as a hat. It was going yellow and crunchy around the edges despite frequent applications of handcream, but the lovingly tended brush of peroxide mohawk was as thick and lustrous as the fur of a pedigree cat.

Trix was twenty-three, lived in the Village, and had three girlfriends and two boyfriends. She was therefore the one who had my missing share of sex, as well as apparently four other people's. She was a little defensive about that, possibly because she was talking to a straight guy with short hair in a suit with a sign floating about his head blaring NO GIRLFRIEND. "Polyamory doesn't mean I'm a slut. It just means I have a lot of love to give and I want a lot of people in my life."

She had problems with men. "Most guys are wired for one-way monogamy. You only sleep with them, but they jump someone else any time a chance to stay in practice raises its head. Plus, I'm very multiple."

"As in . . . ?"

"Multiple orgasms. I get off fast and often. Which means any guy fucking me feels like James Bond. Which means that they don't want anyone else to feel like James Bond."

"Or-gas-em. I've heard of those. Is that with other people?"

She laughed, which I liked. "So tell me what 'the usual' is."

I groaned, checked my glass. Groaned again.

"Vodka later. Talk first. Dish, secret-agent man."

"The usual is that . . . well, I met someone the other day who put it well. I'm a shit magnet."

She arched a drawn eyebrow.

"There are eight bars around this block. I naturally find the one where the barman accessorizes with human headskin. I follow up one lead on this case and I find fifty people furiously masturbating over recut Japanese monster movies." I told her the ostrich story, which had her rolled up with laughter.

"This is just lousy luck, though. It can't happen to you all the time."

"That's the thing. It does. Every case I've had since I opened up business on my own. Never happened when I worked a desk. It's something to do with my direct inter-action with the world. I'm a shit magnet. I'm everything that never happened to anyone else.

"Here's one. I was hired on a missing-persons gig. A sixty-five-year-old terminally ill man had walked out of the hospital and vanished. The family wanted me to find him. Turns out he's joined an old people's suicide club called Sinner's Gate. Sick old people intending to kill themselves to escape indignity. Only Sinner's Gate members believe they led bad lives and have no right to a painless exit.

"I found him in a shithole off the Bowery, in a room with a vacuum cleaner. You know what degloving is?"

She shook her head, nervous of the story.

"I walked in and he put his penis in the vacuum cleaner and switched it on. Ripped the entire skin off his penis instantly. That's degloving. The pain and shock overloaded his nervous system, causing an immediate and massive heart attack that killed him stone dead on the spot."

"Jesus Christ, Mike . . ."

"Big old fat naked dead guy flopped over a vacuum cleaner that was still chewing on his dick. This is my life, Trix."

She looked at me. Direct eye contact, a little creasing of her mouth. I realized it was pity.

"Next round's on me, Mike."

She came back with doubles and sank back into her chair.

"So tell me," I said, absently calculating how much more I should have, "what's NULL stand for?"

"National Union of Lizard Lovers."

"I guess I could have worked that one out."

"And you call yourself a detective. Tell me about this case of yours."

"Promise not to laugh."

"No."

"Okay . . . I've been asked to find an old book that was apparently written by some of the Founders immediately after drafting the Constitution."

"Never heard of it."

"Apparently you weren't supposed to. It was lost from a private collection back in the 1950s and the new holder of the collection wants it back."

"Tell me what this has to do with NULL."

I pulled the black handheld computer from my inside jacket pocket. "According to the very cold trail, NULL obtained it a couple of years ago while blackmailing a mayoral personage, and then traded it to a businessman in return for an infinite lease on that building."

"Not Rudy?" She laughed.

"No idea."

"And you know Donald Trump owns a lot of property in SoHo, right?"

". . . naaah."

She leaned in, grinning. "Damn, this is interesting, though. Where did the book go next?"

I opened the handheld and powered it up. The way she looked at it broke at least two Commandments. "That's one of the new Sonys. You know how much those things cost?"

"Um . . . no. I had a Palm when I was with Pinkerton."

She snatched it off me. The screen lit her eyes like lanterns. "It's got a camera!"

"Where?"

"This lens in the hinge. You didn't see it?"

"I, ah . . . I just thought it was, you know, a high-tech hinge."

Trix smiled at me. "Tard."

Her black fingernail tapped smartly on the screen four times, and then she got out of her chair and crouched next to me. The screen swiveled on a pivot hidden in the hinge, so it was facing us. We appeared in a window on the screen.

"Smile, Mike." A flash went off in the hinge arrangement and a still photo of us resolved on the screen.

In the picture, she's looking at the lens and I'm looking at her.

Trix got up, still clutching the machine. "So your leads are in here?" More tapping brought up the document, and she started paging through it using the Up and Down buttons on the little keyboard in the lower half of the thing.

"This is the coolest thing," she murmured.

"The client gave it to me. It hooks into the net so he can email me updates. Not that I expect any. The trail's all cold. All I can do is pick a point and start following it. Gather as much information as I can along the way."

"You're not going to just jump to the end?"

"My dad had a saying: 'Don't pet a lion until you're damn sure the bastard won't try and eat you.' I want to know what people wanted this book for, and what kind of channels it's being moved along."

"And that's why you were at NULL."

"And now I know. The book is pervert currency."

"'Pervert' is a real pejorative, you know, Mike."

"Hey, I'm from Chicago. In Chicago, perverts are people who don't finish their whiskey and actually sleep with their wives at night."

She gave me a look. "Don't be too sure."

I laughed and polished off my vodka. "What, you want to be my guide to America's deviant underworld?"

Trix looked at me deadpan. "What's the pay?"

"You're serious."

"Sure I'm serious. You need education in the ways of the modern world or else you are frankly doomed. And I can expand my thesis into something killer. I mean, if you just follow the cold trail in here, you're going to be traveling coast-to-coast."

I studied the bottom of my glass.

"I am totally serious, Mike."

"You don't even know me, Trix."

"Mike, you've had five drinks and you haven't even hinted at trying to jump me. If even half of what you've told me about yourself is true, you should've turned into the world's biggest asshole years ago. But you're sweet and you're funny and you don't give up. You know how hard it is, finding someone in this town who's still *determined*?

"And on top of that, life gets interesting around you, I need to write a killer thesis so I can get out of here and do amazing things, and you really, really need some help here."

"This whole 'you're doomed, Mike' thing isn't doing wonders for me, you know . . ."

"Come on, Mike. Let me be your guide to the underworld. Virgil to your Dante."

I really, really did not need to hear that line again.

The bottom of my glass wasn't getting any less empty.

She kept looking at me.

No one had looked at me like I was a ticket to adventure before.

"A hundred dollars a day, and I'll cover travel and accommodation."

Trix's mouth fell open.

"You're kidding me."

"Now I'm the one who's serious."

"Fuck."

"A hundred bucks a day, seven days a week until we're done. Could be a week, could be a month, could be two. Separate rooms, and we're staying in good places. I've got a big expense account, and this is better than me just drinking it all."

She leaned back in her chair. "Wow. That is not exactly what I was expecting."

I felt like a prick for not giving her more than a hundred a day, to be honest. But then I also felt like a prick for buying the company of a smart pretty girl for a few weeks, so it all evened out.

This was, in case you were wondering, literally the only smart move I made during this whole thing.

Chapter 6

I wish I still had that photo.

Chapter 7

I spent Monday and Tuesday buying clothes and luggage and deciding what to do about the gun. I was damned if I was going to drive across America, and besides, that'd mean I'd have to buy a car. But I knew that just wrapping my gun in the gun license and dropping it in a suitcase wasn't going to play. So I ended up packing the license and putting the gun in my office safe.

I considered the gun a professional tool. I'd fired it in anger twice in five years, but if I was honest, I'd have to tell you that I'd threatened people with it more than that.

Plus, I pistol-whipped a tailor once to gain the trust of a disturbed white boy who believed he contained the soul of Huey P. Newton.

So it didn't feel good to lock up the gun. I knew there

was no chance I was going to use it, but it took one option out of the toolbox.

I also had the suspicion, based on nothing at all, that it might freak Trix out a bit.

She met me outside the hotel around noon on Wednesday. The downtown ninjas were doing their level best to chat her up. Trix was showing them her arm tattoos. The cropped top she was wearing showed that they plainly continued on to her chest, and she was teasing them ruthlessly. Most of the ninja swords showed a 45-degree angle.

I came out with my one bag, having decided to travel as lightly as I could. I saw Trix had a single bag, too, which made me smile. "All set, Trix?"

"All ready." She grinned. "You got the tickets?"

I waved them. She turned to the nearest ninja, dipped her chin a bit, and turned big green eyes up at him. "Could we get a cab?"

Four ninjas howled and leapt into Lexington Avenue, waving their swords about. A yellow cab swerved left and clipped one ninja, sending him flying ten feet back to splatter onto the rear of a limo. Another ninja stood and watched in shock, which meant he wasn't going to ninja his way away from the cab, which took him like a mad bull's horns and flipped him over the roof. The cab mounted the sidewalk and jammed on the brakes just as the fender bodyslammed ninja three. The cabbie leaned over and flung open the door, which opened hard on ninja four, batting him down. Scrawled in the dirt on the door were the letters WMD. Inside was an immense black man with an *X* carved into his forehead. Trix and I were the last ones standing. He grinned like a kid at Christmas and yelled, "Where we going, tiny white people?"

Trix and I looked at each other. And then she laughed. "This is just a perfect way to start, Mr. Shit Magnet."

I rolled with it and grabbed the bags. "Newark Airport."

The cab launched off the sidewalk like a cruise missile.

It turned out the cab had two speeds; stop and golike-fuckinghell. The cabbie grappled with his machine like a sumo, wrestling the ballistic cab around corners, great thrusts to the steering wheel to keep the thing on target, slapping it around when it started to fishtail. "You guys look ready for trouble." He laughed. "What's your deal?"

"We're private detectives." Trix grinned. "We're off on a great adventure."

"Private eyes!" He thought this was terrific. He laughed out loud, coughed hard, and punched the steering wheel with a horrible yelp. "You on a case?"

Trix was totally up for this. "Yeah. Some rich guy's

lost a spooky old book and we have to take it away from the weird fuckers who're hiding it."

"Cool! Listen, you know any black private eyes?"

"Sure," I said. "The agency I used to be with had a lot of black guys, a lot of Asian guys, you know?"

"Why ain't they on the TV?"

"Beats the shit out of me."

"Seriously, man. Every time I turn on the TV, it's like *Jones, Freelance Whitey*. Because only middle-aged white guy detectives can fuck shit up, you know what I'm saying? And fucking Quincy, man. There ain't nothing but white guys on that dude's slab. What do they do with the black guys, burn 'em in piles round back?"

"Who's Quincy?" said Trix.

As the cabbie stomped down on the accelerator, I swear I saw the view out the window start distorting.

"It don't matter." The cabbie smiled. "Helter Skelter come soon."

"X'd from society." Trix smiled knowingly.

"Hey! You one hot private eye!"

I made a whatthefuck face at Trix. "Charles Manson," she said. "The *X* on his forehead. It's a Manson thing. Showing their excision from mainstream society. Preparing for Helter Skelter, the race war between whites and blacks that the black people would win."

"You know everything about goddamn Manson but you never heard of Quincy?"

"The thing about Helter Skelter, though, was that Manson considered African Americans to be inferior, and he and his Family would therefore rise from hiding after the war to take over from them. Manson hated black people."

The cabbie laughed a big warm laugh. "Manson was a crazy motherfucker. That don't mean Helter Skelter was a bad idea. I'm just telling his ass—he ain't coming back to take over shit. And there'll be some black private eyes on TV for damn sure."

Trix laughed. I said, "You realize our cabbie is talking about killing us, right?"

The cabbie threw his head back and roared. "You get special dispensation for being cool private eyes. But I'm telling you: be careful out there. Not everyone's as nice as me, you know? Helter Skelter coming. You can see it in everything, man. The weird shit on TV. All that crap on the Internet you hear about. You seen how weird the news is getting? Something's coming, and ain't everyone going to love a private eye when it all starts happening, you know what I'm saying? You guys want Departures, right?"

Yellow cab redshift to Newark Airport.

Chapter 8

Through the airport without any further "magnetism." I figured maybe I'd used up my quota for the day.

"I've never flown before," said Trix, so I made sure she got the window seat. I bought business-class tickets to our first stop, Columbus, Ohio. I'd never been there, but I found myself savoring the normalcy of its name. Columbus, Ohio. It was somewhere from TV weather maps. It made Cleveland sound decadent.

Lots of people in prettily decorated bird-flu masks moved in twitchy flocks around the airport, darting away in migration patterns from anything that coughed.

We were greeted by the plastic grins of flight attendants as we mounted the plane, ushered to big comfortable seats, and given champagne. The grins widened as we finished the first glasses and reached greedily for seconds. Get the passengers smashed and they'll slump quietly throughout the flight. We worked slowly through the second glasses during takeoff, which had Trix plastered to her window wide-eyed and squealing.

The plane banked easy, stepped over the cloud deck, and leveled for Columbus, an hour's run.

An older guy in a short-sleeved shirt with bloodstains on the front sat in the aisle seat next to mine. He gave me a secret little smile. "You know," he said. "You know. If you drink whiskey. And I don't mean a lot of whiskey, just enough to keep the little engines in your head alive. If you drink a bunch of whiskey, you can piss in a cup before you go to sleep. And in the morning all the alcohol will have risen to the surface of the piss. And you can drink it off the top of the piss with a straw."

"I'll, um, I'll certainly bear that one in mind."

He made a happy noise and stuck out a big hand with caked blood all over the fingernails. "Excellent. I'm the pilot."

Trix went white.

Chapter 9

The Columbus airport was one of those places you forget everything about within five minutes of leaving it. We got a cab from there to the hotel I'd booked over the Internet, a place outside the city proper.

Coming out of the airport, we saw a grimy road sign reading, WELCOME TO OHIO, THE BUCKEYE STATE.

Our cabbie had three faded pictures of burly women pasted to the dashboard. Someone had used a marker pen to draw crude knives sticking into their heads and chests. He whispered to himself as he drove, his little fists clenching on the steering wheel.

"What's a buckeye?" Trix asked.

"State symbol kinda thing," the cabbie ground out.

"Yeah, but what's a buckeye?"

He pinned us with red little eyes through the rearview mirror.

"It's a poison nut."

Trix gave me a wry little smile. "That makes sense."

The hotel was a concrete island. Surrounded by highways on all sides. You couldn't walk anywhere from it. The cab dumped us at the front door. The driver was shivering with tension by this point, hissing constantly under his breath, getting close to explosion. I paid the guy a tip. He suddenly glared at Trix and lost it, yelling at the top of his lungs: "They bleed for a week and don't fucking die!"

The cab tore off. I looked at Trix, who just shrugged. "Can't argue with that," she said.

Check-in was unremarkable, and within ten minutes we had our big apartment-style rooms four floors up, complete with exotic widescreen views of the parking lot.

I flicked on the TV for noise while Trix settled in to her room. Some mumbling defective in a cowboy hat was doing a radio talkshow that was inexplicably being televised live. The gig appeared to consist of several perky underachieving assistants doing all the talking while the old guy took his hat off, put it back on, and wondered what the microphone in front of him was for.

There was blood in the toilet, which didn't bother

me as much as it probably should have. I flushed a few times, but it seemed to me that the bottom of the bowl had some kind of wound through which blood continually seeped. There were weird cracks and ripples in the enamel down there. If you squinted through the refraction of the water, the sequence of little lines looked a bit like a hand. I floated some toilet paper over the top and decided to leave it alone.

Trix banged on the door, and sauntered in eating an apple. "It's like housesitting your old-fashioned aunt's place, these rooms." She looked around my room, spotted the little plastic Scotch bottles already drained. "Are you okay, Mike?"

"Fine."

I'd fished the handheld out of my bag already; passed it to Trix. "You want to check out our Columbus lead?"

"Ooh, yeah. Gimme."

She spilled into a chair like a rag doll, holding the apple between her teeth as she clicked the machine open and started thumbing the keyboard.

When she said, "Oh, this is going to be fun," I ordered a full-sized bottle of whiskey from room service.

Chapter 10

Come on over," said the guy on the phone, sounding disturbingly reasonable.

"See?" said Trix, finishing some elaborate eye make-up in the bathroom mirror. The toilet bubbled and hissed behind her. "Physical adventurism doesn't make you an instant freak."

"Did you read this file? Did you read what these people do to themselves? It's a freakshow."

"It's an *interest*. I'm looking forward to meeting the guy."

"For your thesis, right?"

Trix bounced out of the bathroom. Leather boots, flouncy lacy skirt thing, tight top. I decided not to look at her for long.

"Yes, for my thesis. Also because I think he's going

to just be a genuinely interesting guy. Does he know why we're coming?"

I put my hand on my jacket. It seemed heavy. It wanted me to stay right where I was. Stay there, lay down, drink some more, develop some kind of horrific paralysis that prevented me from ever leaving. That required nurses to look after me. Lots of them. With elaborate eye makeup.

I picked up my jacket.

"Yeah, I told him. Figured I may as well be up-front about it. He didn't want to talk about it over the phone."

"Can't argue with that. Are we going?"

I had a rental car waiting outside. It had stained baby clothes and a crack pipe on the backseat. I put my hand inside a plastic bag I found in the glove compartment and carefully lifted them out, dumping it all into a FedEx dropbox outside the hotel lobby. A FedEx employee once tried to steal my breakfast. I hold grudges for decades. Frankly, if I didn't hold grudges, I'd have nothing to play with on Christmas Day.

Trix had gotten the handheld to connect to the Web and produce a road map from the hotel to the location of the man on the phone. I pulled the rental car out of the lot and started following the red line from here to there. Within ten minutes, we were off the highway and barreling up and down leafy suburban hills fringed by big-porched houses stabbed by flagpoles from which bedraggled Stars and Stripes bled.

Trix took it all in like she was riding across the face of the moon. "People really have flags?"

"Sure."

"Now that's weird."

"Yeah, but you're from New York."

"What's that got to do with anything?"

"People in New York are either New Yorkers, or they're Spanish, or Italian, or Irish, or whatever. Who the hell moves to Williamsburg and says, Hey, I'm an *American?* Hell, even after 9/11, if you wanted to tell someone they were being a good guy, people were saying, 'You're a hell of a New Yorker, buddy.'"

"Well, what about you?"

"Well, I'm from Chicago."

Trix snorted.

We nosed out of flag country into parking-lot territory. The standard-issue skyscraper-shape cityscape of Columbus resolved into view, off in the distance. Bland and generic as it was, I wanted to be there. But we had to follow the red line into the tangle of housing out there. To see the man who'd been traded the book for a night of "physical adventurism."

Chapter 11

I parked outside the address, a well-kept place that'd had the front yard cemented over into parking spaces. This was a guy who had a lot of friends. His neighbor had an old Impala rotting in the yard next door. It looked like God had shat in it—the roof punched in, the interior filled with earth and weeds. A brown sneaker poked out of the bottom of the dirt in the doorless passenger side. The sneaker looked worryingly full.

My guy's door chime was blandly anonymous. We waited out there for a couple of minutes, not talking. I was on the verge of giving up when I heard heavy foot-steps inside the house. The door flew open and there was a large mahogany man wearing a purple towel standing there, grinning widely.

"You're the guy who called earlier?"

"Yeah. I'm Mike, this is Trix."

"Yeah? Very cool eye art there, miss. C'mon in. Bit of a rush here."

The air inside was warm and salty. The place was pin-clean and retrotasteful, like someone had embalmed my grandmother's house in 1976. He walked ahead of us, muscles moving under his skin like cats under a satin bedsheet. He was heavily built, and the weird artificial-looking mahogany brought out his muscle definition. He brought us into an old lady's living room, laid a spare towel over the sofa, and sat, inviting us into big arm-chairs that smelled of old potpourri. He gave that big open grin again, big white teeth gleaming in his shaven mahogany head.

"I'm Gary. You got to excuse my look, I just got back from a bodybuilding show. No time to shower."

He pressed his fingertip into his forearm and drew a line down it, exposing white skin.

"Body stain. Brings out the shape under the lights. I compete."

"Did you win?" Trix smiled.

"Ah, second place. Three hundred bucks. I do it for the extra cash, and three hundred's better than a kick in the ass, right? I got this great trainer, English guy, but he's pissed at me because I don't stay in the gym all damn day. He's got this picture he carries around with him from when he competed himself. Him in first place, some other guy in second, Arnold Schwarzenegger in third. He says to me, 'I got first and lived on nothing but fresh pussy for the next two years. Arnie got third and lived in the gym and worked his guts out. And now he's the governor of California and I'm training you, you arsehole.'"

I don't know what was wrong with me. I just wasn't in the mood to make friends. Stupid, really. I was sick of it already, or sick of myself, or all that tangled up together.

"I just want to know where the book is."

Gary grinned that big happy fucking stupid grin, teeth like Scrabble tiles glued into a coffee table. "Sure, I know. Sounds like you guys are on a real weird gig. What is that book, anyway? I mean, the guy told me it was valuable. I did okay out of it—made enough cash to fix up the house and the yard and had a few parties, you know? I'm interested now."

"It was stolen from important people, a long time ago. Where is it?"

"Well, it ain't here. Sold it, like I said."

"Who to?"

"I got a receipt someplace. Damn sure it's not worth the paper it's written on, though, right?" Wide friendly grin. Every time his face gaped open I wanted to break a chair in it.

"Just give me the fucking name."

"Mike," Trix hissed.

The grin shut down like someone threw a switch. "Don't talk to me like that."

"You know what? I just started this case and I'm already sick of uppity perverts. The name."

Gary stood up. He didn't have much height, but he was wide and solid. "Oh, is that what I am? Well, here's the deal, private eye. I'll give you the name. After you've partied with me and my friends a little. Or you can take a walk. Or I can kick your scrawny ass clean from here to the airport and you can fly back to where the weenie vanilla straight boys hide."

The doorbell rang.

"That's my friends," Gary said. "They're bringing the needles."

Big evil grin.

Chapter 12

Eight very large and very gay men filled the living room.

"This is Mike and Trix," said Gary, glowering at me. "Mike wants to have an experience with us."

The tallest man in the room, an Aryan blond in a sprayed-on white T-shirt and bicycle shorts, appraised me without love and then traded looks with Gary. "He's gonna wash first, right?"

"Oh, we're not going to party with Mike. I just want to shoot him up a little, and then he's gonna head back to his hotel."

"Me, too," said Trix. "I mean, I want to play, too."

"You know what we're talking about, right?" Gary said.

"Sure I do. There's some guys in Boston who throw parties and put the photos up on their Web site."

"That's Eugene," a little redhead guy in black jeans

hooted. "I love that guy. Visited him last summer. He took me whale-watching out on Boston Harbor."

"Isn't he cool?" said Trix. "I saw all his photos. Always wanted to try this. I figured that if you infused my labia, it'll feel a little like having balls, you know?"

Feeling vaguely betrayed, I found Gary's eyes and threw my best possible Murderous Gaze into them.

"I'm armed, you know."

"No, you're not."

"What makes you think that?"

"I'm a cop. I can spot a guy carrying from thirty feet."

How badly did I want this job? I could've just walked away from it there and then. Go back to New York, take a partial fee on the case. Hell, take no fee at all, chalk it up to more hideous experience. What fee was worth all this shit?

Trix was watching me. She looked sad. She gave me a little smile, but that was sad, too.

I sat down hard in the chair and dug my fingers into the arms.

"You're not injecting salt water into my testicles and that's that."

Chapter 13

This is where we shoot salt water into your testicles,"
said Gary.

He'd converted a big room in the back of the house
into a huge walk-in shower room, with sound speakers
recessed high in the walls.

"You're going to have to take your clothes off," Gary
observed. "Not that I'm looking forward to seeing you
naked, believe me. You're in shitty shape for a private
detective."

"How many private detectives do you know?"

"Well . . . there's Magnum."

"Get away from me."

"Drop 'em."

"So this is the deal. I let you do this thing to me, and
I get the receipt."

"Right. And quit with the 'do this thing to me' like I'm gonna mutilate you or something. This'll be fun."

"This is what you do for fun?"

"I get some buddies around, we shoot some saline, we have fun. It's a party thing. Play some music, have some drinks, you know. I mean, it's not like we meet in alleyways and mutter, 'wanna do some saline?' It's on the Web, right? Like your girlfriend said."

"She's not my girlfriend."

"You sure?"

"I would have noticed."

He cocked his head to one side. "Huh. Maybe not. She's way cooler than you are. Straight people are so fucking weird."

Aryan Guy came in, stark naked and carrying steaming jugs of water. "Let's give this guy some balls," he laughed.

Trix followed him in, holding a medical bag. She winked at me. "I want to see this."

"I'm your fucking thesis now?"

"You need to relax," she said, handing Gary the bag. "This is going to be a new experience for you. Just enjoy it for what it is."

"It's being trapped in a shower with a gay cop who wants to mutate my nuts, Trix."

"Oh, will you unclench? Now get 'em off."

"Gary, does she have to be here?"

"Trix wants to be here, man."

"I don't want her to see me naked."

"Dude, none of us *wants* to see you naked."

"You don't want me to see you naked?"

I couldn't judge from her voice what she really meant by that. Or possibly what I wanted her to mean by that.

"Listen," I said to Gary, "I'm her employer. It doesn't seem . . . appropriate."

Trix gave an explosive sigh. "God, I hate that word. 'Appropriate.' It's like, hang a sign around my neck reading I Am a Boring Asshole. Okay, whatever, I'll go."

She stomped out, and I felt worse. Aryan Guy stood in front of me and folded his arms. "If you're done shitting on your girl and generally dicking around, take off your clothes and we'll all try real hard not to vomit on you. Now."

I stripped, picturing their corpses being eaten by weasels.

"Jesus," Aryan Guy said. "Last time I saw a body like yours it was dangling from a tree on *CSI*. Do you live on grease sucked straight out of burger-joint drains or something? I bet the only exercise you get is flushing the toilet."

"Oh, shut up."

"Seriously, man. You're like two steps from the grave-yard."

"I have a rough life. My girlfriend left me for a transgendered dyke with hair implants in her nipples."

"And alarm bells should have been going off right there, man."

There was a burst of laughter from the living room, and Scandinavian pop started bubbling out of the speakers.

"There we go." Gary grinned, his hand in the black bag. "Now we're having fun." He split an IV tube out of its sterile wrapper.

"Look, I'm sorry I got in your face before. I'm not having a good time here."

"Well, now you're gonna have some fun."

Chapter 14

Gary flicked on the showers, and I was doused in warm water.

"Relax," said Gary. "It makes your balls more pliable."

My balls felt like they'd climbed back up into my body and made a nest under my lungs.

"You people really do this for fun?"

"Man, you are *such* an asshole. Listen, when you were a kid, did you ever spin round and round on the spot until you were dizzy?"

"Sure."

"Why?"

"Well . . . because I liked the feeling, I guess. Yeah, okay, I can see where this is going . . ."

"So don't be such a jerk about it. We like the feeling. It's different, it doesn't hurt anybody, and it goes away."

"It does go away?" I actually said that twice—the second time I got the borderline-hysterical squeak out of my voice.

"Oh my God," groaned Gary. "Were you raised by nuns or something? I figure you're warm enough. Let's go. Step out of the water."

He kept the water running; soft blankets of steam wrapped around me as I stood and faced my certain testicular doom. Gary crouched in front of me, and I fought not to flinch as he gently stroked one of my balls with a fingertip.

"We should have shaved you. You've got a bush like a seventies porn star down here, princess."

"I hate you worse than Osama," I hissed.

Gary laughed out loud. "You are just too easy to freak out, you know that?" And then he jabbed the IV needle into my nuts.

While I was yelping, Gary followed the tube back to one of the water jugs, and lifted out the warmed saline pack it was connected to. He held it up, and—Christ, I still grit my teeth and cross my legs just thinking about it—something awful with weight and temperature started flowing into my balls.

I grunted and twisted around on my feet. "Will you relax?" snapped Gary. "Anyone would think I was poisoning you."

"Hhmmnrrgg" was about the cleverest response I could manage at that point. I knew I was wobbling. My testicles were flushed with heat, and getting heavier. I looked down out of one eye. My testicles were the size of a champion prize-grown onion I'd seen at a market gardening competition as a kid. And expanding. I shut my eye again, tight. It felt like I was smuggling cannonballs in my scrotum.

"I can't believe someone can be as tense as you and not die of something bursting," Gary commented. "You need to get laid more than any human or animal I've ever met."

"I don't think there's much chance of that happening ever again," I ground out between gritted teeth. "And I have a feeling kids are out of the picture now, too. You've cooked my guys."

"I may have done the world a favor," he said thoughtfully.

After what seemed like ten or eleven years, the flow finally stopped. Gary expertly yanked out the IV and thumbed a small, round adhesive dressing onto the puncture. The brine in my testicles rippled horribly. "That's pretty good," he observed. "Take a look."

I unclenched one eye again, swiveled it down, and screamed.

Chapter 15

Gary gave me a big blue towel, wrapped it around my waist as if he were dressing a child, and led shaky me back into the living room.

"Well, Magnum here took it kind of like a man. He's got balls now."

There was hooting and clapping, none of which I felt was especially kind.

Trix said, "You really did it?"

Gary laughed. "Sure he did." And ripped the towel off me.

It looked like someone had nailed a basketball to me.

"That's *awesome*," Trix trilled, clapping some more. I had five seconds of feeling absurdly proud. Before, you know, realizing I was standing naked in front of Trix with mutated testicles and understanding that it pleased her in some way. At which point I grabbed the towel back and lashed it around me.

Aryan Guy grinned. "Either he likes me, or he likes her."

And, oh God, she smiled at me.

I turned to Gary. "Clothes. Receipt."

Gary sighed. "Clothes are in the next room, the guest bedroom. Receipt and some notes on what I remember about the guy are on top of them. Lots of luck, Magnum."

I moved to leave the room. Trix yelled, "My turn!"

I saw Gary react. "You sure?"

"I want balls now!" She giggled. "Mike, stay a while. I want to try."

I felt eight kinds of weird, and it was exhausting. "I'll wait for you in the car," I said, and went into the other room, shutting the door on them.

The notes were cop notes, fragmented but comprehensible as a pen-portrait. They and the receipt did not fill me with pleasure. My crappy luck was holding on like a son of a bitch.

As I realized when I looked at the neatly folded pile of my clothes on the bed.

My pants were, of course, built for a man with normal testicles.

I sat down gently on the edge of the bed and tried very hard not to cry.

With my testicles laying on top of my legs.

The music got louder. I could hear laughing, and clapping.

I almost broke my back leaning over to pull my socks on. No way in hell I was going to attempt to get the underpants on. I'd go commando and take excruciating care with the zipper. The shirt was easy enough, but the main event was obviously going to be my pants. I awkwardly wrestled my feet through the pants legs, scrunching the thing down, and then lay back on the bed. I was suddenly reminded of a girlfriend from back when I was in my teens: watching her lean back and hump and writhe into a pair of stretch jeans, and thinking, Christ, she looks good in them and all, but is it really worth all that performance?

Ho ho. Of course she wasn't going to leave the house with her bits out in the open air. And neither was I. I hooked my fingers into the belt loops and dragged the pants up me an inch at a time. I told myself I was doing fine. Roomy pants. Not even a remote possibility that my balls were so grotesquely inflated that they couldn't be packed inside. Hitching them up another inch. There we go, Mike. An inch over your nuts, you clever bastard you. Eeek. Cold zipper metal where it really really should never ever be. Lift up your ass, buy a little wiggle room . . .

I got the top of my pants to fasten, and bent forward to see how I was doing.

My general front-of-pants area looked like a watermelon stuffed in a kangaroo pouch. I could forget zipping myself up. But I found that if I left my shirt untucked, it draped over my testicles pretty well. Excellent. Jacket on, paperwork in pockets, and I was ready to go. I stood up and groaned. They felt heavier than ever before. Heading for the door, I was waddling more than walking, and I began to worry that this wasn't going to work.

The side of the house I was in was empty. Everyone was in the shower room, and having a wild old time by the sound of it. I waddled to the front door, my pants pressing hard enough on my balls to start me feeling sick. But I just had to get to the car. I got out the door, shut it behind me quietly, and my pants fastening burst.

Early evening had set in. Lights were on in all the houses. Dogfight noises were coming from the neighbor's place. I could hear kids playing down the street, and the game sounded like it involved death of some kind.

I held on to my pants with my left hand, and lifted my scrotum with the other. Carrying my testicles, I walked to the car as fast as I could. Which, you know, wasn't as fast as all that.

I don't like to think about what I looked like, hefting my own gonads down the front yard path to my car. I thought, in those slow painful moments, that I'd finally hit bottom.

Which was just fucking stupid, really.

Chapter 16

I found that I had to kind of limbo into my car, leaning back and almost heaving my hideous genital weight in ahead of me.

With the car door shut and my scrotum on my lap, I sighed, switched the car radio on, and settled down to wait for Trix. Looking at my watch. Looking out the window. Wondering exactly how long it took to inflate a woman's labia until they passed as gonads. Minutes crawled.

Pressing buttons at random found me something that sweetly declared itself to be "Ohio's Liberal Voice," but what followed appeared to be nothing but a recording of someone screaming at a very high pitch for a very long time.

I stabbed the deck some more, cycling through a soft-rock station, some weird broadcast of a woman doing nothing but reading numbers very slowly, and what I guessed was a local church channel. A man was explaining in a very loud voice, as if speaking to a child, that everyone in California likes anal sex. "I like churches. They like anal sex. I like families and children. They like having abortions. No, it's true. They are all secular Jews who hate Jesus and America. And they call me a Nazi when I say that. But let me say this. Hitler was always very respectful of the church. And he *hated* cigarettes."

An announcer's voice came in to tell me that I'd been listening to Proinsias Kernahan, president of the Catholic League, and to ask me to wait until after these messages to hear the rest of the evening news. Dear God, but it was time for a cigarette. I punched the search button again, fished out a half-crushed pack of Dunhills, and lit up with relief. The radio scanned around a bit and landed on something that sounded oddly amateur. Listening and smoking, I came to understand it was a micropower radio station. A couple of kids broadcasting out of a back room somewhere. And somewhere close by, too. The kids, only one of whom sounded hopelessly stoned, explained that their signal didn't reach more than a couple of miles, and even that only if the wind was behind it and you were standing downhill with your arms out and a wire coat hanger stuck on top of your head.

The unstoned one was pretty smart. In between the music—which apparently was all by local unsigned bands, and some of it wasn't bad—he talked about what they were doing and why. By playing local indie music, they were both supporting his community and broadcasting donated content that didn't require a royalty payment. They weren't, they insisted, pirates. They were even observing band adjacency, he said—this one, the guy who hadn't smoked a field of weed, was obviously the Head Geek—broadcasting on 94.2, clear space between two "lite"/soft-rock channels. And that was the point, he figured—most of Columbus's dial was all eaten up by soft rock, country, and Christian radio. All the major monolithic radio entities ran stations in Columbus, but they all broadcast exactly the same kind of material. They *all* had a Christian station, they all had anesthetic adult easy-listening rock stations playing the kinds of records we used to lift out of our parents' collections and use as ashtrays when I was a kid.

It suddenly occurred to me: I didn't remember the last time I went to a gig. Couldn't remember the last time I heard live music. Or went to a club to hear a DJ.

They played something by another local group, that had the real thump and clang of live music. The drummer started up on the toms, and collapsed into a glorious mess that sounded like he'd kicked the drumkit down a flight of stairs. The bass walked in and made the back of the car rattle. The lead guitarist went screaming down the strings and I laughed out loud, it sounded so good. And then there was a fuckload of static, ten seconds of silence, and a fight. Someone had entered their make-shift recording studio, and one of the kids, probably the smart one, had put the microphone back on.

"We are the FCC," a loud voice proclaimed. "Take off your clothes and put these orange jumpsuits on."

"The fuck?" said Herb Boy.

"Pirate radio operations have been reclassified as Broadcast Terrorism. You're going to be wearing dogs in your asses at Abu Ghraib for the next five years, you dirty bastards."

"This is community radio!"

"If we wanted communities, we'd make Clear Channel pay us to run them. Put on the hoods, too. No more devil music for you, Radio bin Laden."

I switched off the radio, miserably, wondering if it was all my fault for listening and daring to enjoy it.

I got a little angry.

Not long after, the passenger-side door opened, and Trix climbed in, grinning.

I took a deep breath and said, "All set?"

"Sure. You should have stayed." She looked at the dashboard. "What happened to the radio?"

"It broke."

"Looks like someone kicked it in. Did someone break into the car?"

"Must've." I started up the car. "Let's go. I need to buy plane tickets."

"Where are we going?"

"Texas," I grunted.

She looked at me. Up. And down. And giggled. "Well, they do say everything is bigger there."

"Oh, ha fucking ha." I went to adjust my shirt. And found that things had changed.

I guess I'd been in the car a couple of hours. My balls had diminished to an approximation of their standard size. My penis, however, was significantly bigger than I was used to. Like half a dozen times. And, not having rearranged my shirt, I found that I was sticking out of my pants like I was an incompetent salami smuggler.

"They told me that the saline diffuses out in an hour or two," Trix said. "I guess it migrates on the way."

She leaned in way too close and whispered, "If that happens to me, my clit is going to look like a pool ball."

I threw the gearshift and gunned the engine. "You better get some sleep. Neither of us are going to be laying on our fronts tonight."

"I don't mind you laying on your back," Trix said.

"I'm going to order plane tickets and make a phone

call, and then I'm going to get so drunk that I cannot see. You can find something to do tonight, right?"

"Sure. I'm going to jerk off like a freak. Want to watch?"

"Jesus, Trix . . ."

"What is wrong with you, Mike?"

"Me?"

"Yes, you! I'm all tingly as hell, I'm hornier than a dozen rabbits, I've seen you looking at me, and suddenly you're a monk. Are you scared of me?"

"Of course I'm not goddamn scared of you."

"Well, you're pissing me off, anyway. You want me to go home tomorrow?"

"You want me to buy you a ticket home?"

"That's not what I asked. Do you want me to go?"

"I'll buy you a ticket home, if you want."

"What are you, eight? Answer the question, Mike."

"No."

"Christ! What no? No to me leaving?"

"No, I'm not eight."

"Mike, I could snap your neck using only my pussy lips right now."

"Oh, for . . ."

I pulled the car over, in sight of the highway back to the hotel.

"Trix . . . No, I don't want you to go. If I've been shit

at hiding that I look at you sometimes, then I'm sorry. I never meant to make you feel uncomfortable. If you want to go because I'm being creepy, then I'll buy you a ticket, pay you for your time, and we're cool. And I'm sorry. Okay?"

Trix sighed. Looked out the window. Looked back at me.

"Mike. I am asking you to have sex with me."

". . . oh."

"Oh? Did the easy-reading version work?"

Chapter 17

If you think I'm telling you about having sex with Trix, you're insane.

Chapter 18

I think it's finally going down," Trix said.

I took a look. "Yeah. You no longer have girl-balls."

She gave that little tinkling giggle and snuggled into my arm. "I have decided that we need to do that more often."

"Fill our bits with salty water?"

She bit my nipple. "No. The other thing. Although, you know . . ."

"No chance. One-time thing. I'm not carrying my nuts around in a wheelbarrow for you."

"And I thought you liked me. Didn't you have to make a phone call?"

"Shit. So I did. Someone distracted me."

"So it's all my fault now?"

"Absolutely." I kissed her hair. "I'll call him later. He'll still be awake."

"Who do you need to talk to?"

"Bob Ajax. Guy I knew back in my Chicago days. He moved to San Antonio a few years ago. A little local knowledge might help."

"You don't look happy about it."

"Oh, I like Bob fine. He's a good guy. What bothers me is who we have to go and see." I sighed, tried to relax. "Doesn't matter. Not right now."

"No. It doesn't. You stay right here. How long since you last got laid?"

"Well, I remember saying, Mr. Lincoln, when am I going to meet a nice girl?"

"Seriously."

"Since my girlfriend left me, pretty much. A few years."

"You're kidding."

"I wish."

"A few years? I would have died. It would have healed over."

"If you check the condom, you'll find a bunch of gray pebbles in the end."

"Oh, that's gross."

"You bring out the best in me. I need a cigarette."

Cold and sticky, wobbly knees, rooting around in my jacket, something occurred to me. Because I can't just leave things alone.

"Why?"

"Why what?"

"Why this."

She coiled around onto her front, feet on the headboard, and considered me. "I think I want to meet your ex. And kill her for whatever she did to your brain."

"No, really. Was it just because . . . ?"

"Because what? Because your dick was full of brine? Because when I'm horny I just jump into bed with the first available live body?"

"No," I lied, because when she put it like that I sounded like an asshole, and that couldn't be right. "I just . . . You weren't interested in me like . . . that."

She stared. "Oh my God, Mike."

"What? You came for the thesis and the job. I know that. That was the deal, I'm not pissed or anything."

Her eyes were like saucers. "You. Are. Such. A. Retard."

"What did I do now?"

"Mike. I wanted to kiss you the first time you made me laugh. But you're always so . . . freaked out. By *everything*. Mike, you're a really nice guy who made me laugh and you wanted me to go on an *adventure* with you. You think that happens to me, you know, *ever*? Do you have any idea when anyone last wanted to talk to me for what was in my *head*?"

I stood there like an idiot with the cigarettes in my hand, unable to think of anything worth saying.

"I'm not getting through to you, am I?" Trix smiled.

". . . um."

"Okay. Easy-reading version. I wanted to spend time with you and see what happened. I am kind of a big slut, but I don't give it away for candy bars. I sleep with people I really like. I really like you. I am not here for the money or the thesis. I am here because I really like you, and because you took me on an adventure with you. How's that?"

". . . big slut?"

"Come here."

I went back to the bed, forgetting the smokes. She reached up, grabbed me by my nipple, and pulled me down.

"Here's what's going to happen. We are going to continue our trip for as long as it lasts. We are going to learn about each other and be together. We are going to be friends. We will go back to New York and we will still be friends. And we are going to have sex, you know, a *lot*. Because that's what I do with my very best friends because it makes us closer and because it is fun. You will agree now."

"Yes."

"There. See how easy that was?" She flipped me onto my back and looked at me thoughtfully. "Hm. We may need some ropes."

". . . oh my God."

"God can't help you now, Mike. There's only me here."

Chapter 19

Bob? It's Mike McGill."

Bob had acquired a bit of Texas in his accent.

"Mike! Jesus, man, it's been years! How you been?"

"I followed you out of Chicago. Set up on my own in New York."

"Good for you, man. Always said you were the smartest guy in the agency. So what's up?"

"You still in San Antonio?"

He laughed. The laugh had a bit of edge in it. I filed that away, nervously.

"Sure. You need something?"

"Listen, me and my partner need to fly down there today and do some digging. Any chance you could give us some local knowledge?"

"Damn, I'll pick you up at the airport. Got a flight yet?"

I'd already booked tickets by phone, and gave him the details. That was that, and we hung up.

"Huh," I said, standing over the phone.

"Problems?" Trix said from the bathroom.

"I don't know. He didn't sound right."

"Define."

"Nothing ever got to Bob. He was Teflon—everything just slid right off him. Stuff only ever came out when he was drunk. He sounded . . . not stressed, but edgy. Not like Bob."

"Been a while since you saw him, though, right? I think I like being your partner, by the way."

"Well, what the hell else was I going to call you? I couldn't tell him you were my girlfriend or anything."

Waited.

"No, you couldn't," came her voice.

Shit.

"Friend-with-benefits doesn't sound too professional, either," she laughed. Making damn sure I had no idea where things stood.

She tripped out of the bathroom, flames around her eyes. "So what's the plan, boss?"

"Bob'll pick us up, we'll find a hotel, and he'll give us some background on the next visit."

"Which is?"

"Ever heard of Roanoke Oil?"

Her face set. "Yes, I have. Serious eco-criminals."

"I didn't know that. Well, we're going to have some fun. Because the thing was bought from our briny friends by the Roanoke family."

"Oh, wow. That's interesting. How long ago?"

"Three years, I think."

"Wow. You know one of the Roanokes tried to take a stab at the presidency last time around?"

A few things went click click click in my head. And, I don't know, call it an aftereffect of the exfiltration of vintage semen, call it suddenly becoming uncomfortable with only ever having told her part of the story, call it what you fucking like, I don't care. But I asked her to sit down, and I told her what the book really was. Told her what I'd been told it was and what it was for.

After a while, she blew out a breath and said, "Holy shit."

"Yeah."

"Holy *shit*."

"You said that."

"What do you think he wants it back for?"

"Well, I don't think it's a magic book. I think it's a little bit of history that he wants safely swept under his own carpet, rather than floating around out in the world."

Trix stood up. Sat down again. Thought for a moment. Stood up. "Can I have one of your cigarettes?"

I handed her the pack and the lighter. There was memory in her fingers as she lit up. I felt bad for bringing on a relapse. She sucked the smoke down, and coughed it back out in big blue puffs. "What the fuck are these?"

"They're organic."

She looked at the pack. "You smoke cigarettes called 'American Ghost'? Jesus, Mike. Organic *what*? Dead bodies?"

"Feeling better?"

"No!"

"Oh."

She stabbed the cigarette to death in the ashtray. "Mike, I'm working for the White House."

"It's an *adventure*."

"It's the *government*."

"It's their money we're spending. It's their money I'm giving you. They are paying for our *adventure* because, well, they're nuts and they think there's a magic book on the loose in America. It's not a magic book. It's a faintly embarrassing antique that they are handing over stupid amounts of money for me to attempt to return to them. That said—"

Trix found my eyes. "—that *said*, one of the Roanokes tried to take a stab at the presidency last time around."

"Yeah. So you said. What happened?"

"The guy couldn't get on the ballots. Had worse problems than Nader. Spent a lot of money, but it all fell apart. Indymedia called it Bush Envy. See, what threw people was that he had no experience at all, in anything. He made Ross Perot look like JFK, you know? No one knew what made him think he could win. But, what I'm now thinking *is*, see, if he had the thing, the book, an actual honest-to-God whole other draft of the Constitution . . ."

"Yeah."

"*Yeah*. If he'd managed to get into the political fight, he could have, I don't know, shown it off, or used it as secret leverage . . ."

"Hold on." I quickly lit myself a cigarette. "You're a bit ahead of me. Mentioning him running for office, that put up the red flag, because it's the first political connection to the book I've had so far. But you think it could actually leverage someone into office?"

"Don't know. I mean, if your guy honestly believes it's full of . . . what? Precepts by which America can be healed? If your guy believes it, maybe someone else is crazy enough to. A book that can save America, signed by all the Founders . . ."

". . . hell. That's interesting. That's really interesting. We need to get on a plane."

"Hell, yeah," she said.

Chapter 20

At the departure gate, a drunken airport security woman was handing out box cutters to the passengers.

"My asshole boyfriend's in San Antone," she slurred, pressing the plastic handle, sticky with beery sweat, into my hand. "Take over the plane, drop it on the fucking Alamo."

Trix and I dropped the things into the nearest wastebasket. I looked back to see a team of cops lay into her with batons. "I'm white, you bastards!" she yelled, until one of them shot her with a Taser. The cops gathered around and silently watched her flop around on the floor like a fish out of water.

"Just another day out at the zoo," Trix whispered. "Keep walking, Mike."

Chapter 21

Bob Ajax was waiting for us in the arrivals lounge at the San Antonio airport. Huge and fifty, with a grin like he'd just cheated God out of his savings.

"Mike Mc fucking Gill," he bellowed. "Man, you've lost weight. New York City must be killing you."

"Look at your goddamn stomach, man. You eat your last wife or something?"

"Bastard. And I see you're hanging out with a better class of person these days."

Trix read him in a second and gave him a sexy crooked smile. "Trix Holmes. Mike's assistant."

"Hell. I could use an assistant like you."

"You couldn't afford me, Bob."

Bob laughed out loud. He'd always liked women who'd talk back to him just a little bit. "Girls with balls" were good. Women with an actual mind of their own who could prove him wrong in something were, of course, castrating bitches who should be drowned in bottomless wells. He'd heard of a place in Iceland where troublesome women were in fact drowned in a freezing bottomless well. Bob had once gotten inhumanly drunk and attempted to dig such a well outside the office in Chicago, using a stolen pneumatic drill and, in the final moments of his excavation, the head of a passing police officer. I helped him keep his job in the aftermath, and we'd been solid friends ever since.

Bob was still driving the same car: an immense, battered old Lincoln Continental that was held together by spit and a prayer. He slung our bags in a trunk already half-full with, in Bob's words, "tools of the trade," and then wrestled himself behind the wheel.

"One of those things looked like a harpoon, Bob. You do much whaling in San Antonio?"

"It's a Persuader. Punches out door locks. Tool of the trade. You see the big black tube next to it?"

"Yeah."

"*That's* the harpoon gun. Not loaded. Need to buy more 'poons. Because, y'know, I'm not as young as I was, and some of these bastards can run fast."

"You harpoon people?"

"A bit."

The Lincoln coughed and rolled out of the airport parking lot. It was warm, and the air conditioning smelled like something small and furry was trapped inside it, so I settled for rolling down the window.

"Yeah, sorry," Bob said, reading my face in the rearview mirror. "There's a rat stuck in here someplace. Little fuck is waiting for me to show weakness. He don't know Bob Ajax."

"Rats do that. How long to the hotel?"

"Forty minutes. So tell me about this job."

"Short version? Mad old rich guy in D.C. lost an antique book, hired me to recover it. The paper trail led us down here. The Roanoke family."

"Well," Bob said, "I didn't want to talk about it too much on an open line. But this might be the end of the road for you."

Trix leapt on that. "Open line?"

"Damn right," Bob shrugged. "You don't screw around where the Roanokes are concerned. The two most dangerous things in the world are rich people and crazy people. The Roanokes are rich like pharaohs and crazier'n a snake-fucking baby."

Trix shot me a look. I didn't react. I knew Bob. And sure enough, his eyes were flicking to the rearview mirror, watching us. His shoulders tensed up.

"They have the wrong kind of friends all over Texas,

lady," Bob growled. "People owe them. They understand the modern kind of power. They don't stand on high and wait for people to bring tribute. They spend their money and make sure everyone owes them something. You think people like that ever have less than a thousand wiretaps running at any one time?"

Looking absently out the window, I reached down and across, found Trix's hand, and gave it a single sharp squeeze.

"I guess you're right," Trix said.

"Damn right," Bob said, visibly relaxing.

"How long to the hotel, again?" Trix sighed.

Blank highway broke up into factories, housing, parking lots, stores. It didn't look much different from Columbus. The press of cars grew tighter. Not a human body to be seen on the streets, such as they were.

"Does nobody walk here, or what?"

"Ah, well, you've come here at an exciting time, Mike. There's a surplus in the city budget this year, so you know what we're gonna do? We're gonna pour us some sidewalks!"

"No sidewalks," Trix muttered. Trying out the phrase on her tongue.

"You East Coast types," Bob smirked. "You're like little weakass colonies on the edge of Real America, you know that?"

"Walking makes us weakass?" I laughed.

"Fine for your cramped little towns like New York," Bob proclaimed, sitting up taller in his seat. "But this is the big country, and we need big cars, and the space for 'em. This sidewalk thing, it just means we ain't too proud to make things a little easier for our visiting cousins from Weakass Country. We're big people like that."

"You're from fucking Minneapolis."

"Texans are born, and Texans are grown, and they're all Texans nonetheless. I fucking love it here."

A few minutes later, he started crying, and had to pull over the car.

"They hate me," he gasped between great painful heaving sobs, his big soft face contorted in agony. "God help me, Mike, they all fucking hate me like I was Hitler's fartcatcher."

Chapter 22

Bob refused to talk about it. Drove us to the hotel in stony silence, told us he'd pick us up at eight for dinner, tore off at high speed.

The hotel was expensive, because I felt like it. And this time I had arranged for a single suite, rather than two rooms. Trix didn't say a thing, as we entered the room. Just smiled and raided the minibar.

Shoes off and feet up and drinks and smiling at each other, and life was pretty good.

"So," Trix said. "Your friend Bob."

"He's gone completely nuts."

"That was my educated opinion, yeah. What happened?"

"You know as much as I do. Haven't spoken to the guy in ages. He could be a little odd when he was drinking, but nothing like this. Bob was a hardass. That whole thing in the car, I have no idea where that came from. He's gotten into trouble down here, I guess." I sighed, stretched. "I don't think I want to know what kind of trouble."

"You want to go out?"

"Dinner's in four hours."

"C'mon, Mike. We can't see America from hotel rooms."

"Sure you can. Window's right over there."

"You know what I mean. C'mon. There's all those weirdo Texans out there to gawp at."

"For someone who plays Champion to Perverts as much as you do, you're awfully dismissive of the great state of Texas."

"Oh, give me a break. This is Jesusland. Red State. Ma Ferguson country."

"Who?"

"Mike, you are a cultural void."

"Probably. Who?"

"Ma Ferguson. Governor of Texas back in the 1920s. When someone tried to get Spanish taught in schools, you know what she said? 'If English was good enough for Jesus Christ, then it's good enough for Texas!' Mike, these are the people who want to put people like me in prison."

I finished my drink. Smiled sweetly. "Miriam Amanda Ferguson, young lady. She ran as an anti-Klan candidate at a time when there were almost half a million Klan members in Texas. Pardoned two thousand prisoners."

Trix frowned. "You're kidding me."

I jerked a thumb at the window. "1939, a civil rights leader gave a speech here in San Antonio, given legal coverage by the mayor. The Klan arranged a riot, and tried to kill the mayor. Not long after, the Klan were burned out of San Antonio and haven't had a building here since. You know the mayor's name?"

"You're going to tell me. You're enjoying this too much not to."

"Mayor Maverick."

I enjoyed the face she made.

"Couldn't make this stuff up, could you?"

"What's your point?"

"My point. Yes. My point is that people are the same all over. It's not like you're flying into a jungle when you go south. Texans, Minnesotans, Montanans, other 'ans' beginning with Ts and Ms—all the goddamn same, same mix of heroes and pricks, same old bunch of nice and nasty."

"And this is your motivation for not wanting to go out for a walk? That it's all the same out there?"

"Yep."

"You're a lazy bastard."

"That, too. But your whole Us-and-Them Thing doesn't work when it's all Us."

"But mostly you're a lazy bastard."

"Yep."

"How the hell did you know that, anyway?"

"Way back when I was working at Pinkerton, I had to update an in-house dossier on the Klan. I used to be kind of thorough, and stuff sticks in my head. You know that in some places the Klan became general moral guardians and started flaying white men for getting divorces?"

"Is your head just filled with useless information?"

"Like you wouldn't believe. Okay." I struggled up out of my chair. "Let's go see the Alamo. Apparently it's never been the same since Ozzy Osbourne pissed on it."

"Ozzy Osbourne's funny. He never really did that, right? It's like the story about the bat."

"Nope. Ozzy Osbourne pissed on the Alamo. But he wasn't wearing a dress. However, I happen to know that he got the soft treatment. Two-hundred-buck fine for public intoxication. But he actually committed a crime called desecration of a venerated object, because the Alamo is officially a shrine. Should've gotten a year in prison."

"You're trying to bore me into a coma so you don't have to go out, aren't you?"

"Yes. Let me tell you about the rogue Judas tribe of Native Americans, the Potowatomi, who sided with the French and the British before coming to Texas—"

"Fine, fine, I'll watch some television—"

"But you know? If you look closely at the front of the Alamo, the top-right area, you can see where the numbers 666 have become visible on the brick since Ozzy pissed on the building. But you want to watch television. That's fine. It'll keep."

Trix hit me with lots of things.

Chapter 23

And to make up for being an asshole, I had to buy her some clothes.

We were going out to dinner, and she was worried about Bob. More worried than I was, I realize now, or perhaps just more sensitive to his touch of crazy. I think I just wanted to keep thinking of him as Teflon Bob. So she didn't want to wear anything that might stand out in what she felt was an essentially conservative town. Didn't want to make Bob uncomfortable. And I, apparently, needed to be punished for trying to educate her.

Not that I was doing anything of the sort. I was just being an asshole. So we shopped for clothes.

Shopping for clothes is a Boyfriend Thing. You stand around and look blankly at a bunch of pieces of fabric and you look at the price tags and you wonder how something that'd barely cover your right nut can cost the price of a kidney and you watch the shop assistants check you out and wonder what you're doing with her because she's cute and you're kind of funny-looking and she tries clothes on and you look at her ass in a dozen different items that all look exactly the same and let's face it you're just looking at her ass anyway and it all blurs together and then someone sticks a vacuum cleaner in your wallet and vacuums out all the cash and you leave the store with one bag that's so small that mice couldn't fuck in it. Repeat a dozen times or until the front of your brain dies.

Point being: it's a Boyfriend Thing. And it's not just you, the Boy, who thinks so. Every shop assistant on the way will assume you're the Boyfriend.

Especially with the laughing and the teasing and the hugging and the kissing and the holding of hands. And the carrying of bags. Very Boyfriend Thing.

The United States government bought Trix quite a lot of clothes.

I hope it's clear that I was really, really trying not to be weird about the way things were. All the time, I was telling myself, just enjoy it for what it is, don't be weird, don't get all screwed up over something it isn't. The usual mantra when you're with someone who you're not really with and desperately want to be.

Have you noticed how telling yourself all that shit never actually helps?

Chapter 24

Bob picked us up outside our hotel, wearing his Same Old Bob face, not a hint of his earlier breakdown. I decided not to push it, and Trix read me. She was wearing tight black things: still very much her, but covering her tattoos, and had traded her boots for kitten heels. "You know he's going to be looking to see what anyone thinks of him," she'd said to me. "Why make it hard for him? It's not like I'm swapping my brain for a Stepford Wife's. You need his help, right? So let's not give him anything to freak out over."

For my part, I was just hoping for a quiet night.

The steakhouse was called Ma's Place.

"Take it easy," Trix whispered as I tensed up. "Just a coincidence."

"It's a sign from God that he's going to shit on my dinner."

"No such thing as God. You relax, too. I don't want to have to manage two freaked-out men tonight."

"I'll have the Special." Bob grinned at the waitress, spreading out in his chair.

"You sure?" said the waitress, eyeing him dubiously. With one eye, as the other was under an eyepatch. I saw Trix looking at the tattoo on the waitress's forearm, which, in blotchy bluish letters, read SKEETER.

"Hell, yes." Bob laughed. The Texas in his accent got stronger. "Been a busy day, and a man needs steak."

"If you're sure," she muttered, and turned to Trix and me. We were still working our way through the menu. "Any vegetarian options?" Trix asked. "I don't eat a lot of meat."

"This is a steakhouse, ma'am," the waitress hissed. "If it don't come off a cow, we don't sell it."

"There's a ladies' option," Bob said, trying to be helpful.

Trix caught a swearword in her mouth before it came out. Swallowed it and gave up a "that'll be fine. Medium? With a salad?"

"No salad. Cows only shit salad, ma'am."

Trix laughed. "Okay. The small portion of fries, then. Mike?"

"Jesus." I scanned the menu hopelessly. It was all dish names, rather than useful descriptions. "Um . . . Rump steak? Well done. Some fries?"

"So that's one Special, one Ma's Dainty Plate, and one Cattle Mutilation, ruined. Drinks?"

"Ma's Dainty Plate?" Trix scowled as the waitress rolled off. "I should've had the Special."

"The Special's for men only. Says on the menu," said Bob, flapping the damp cardboard pamphlet at us. "See? 'The Special—For Men.'"

"You get a club to kill it with, too?" Trix said, deeply unimpressed.

"I wish!" Bob laughed. The waitress returned with drinks. I reached for beer like a drowning man. Not that drowning men tend to want beer. You know what I mean.

Bob was given a veritable pot of iced tea. It was so full of sugar that the straw stood up. You could see Bob's chest laboring to suck the stuff up into his head. The surface of the drink moved in slow viscous waves, like a lake of tar.

Bob sighed and belched. "I tell you," he smiled, "when you find a place in this town that does good iced tea, you stick to it like glue. So. Let's talk about your case."

Again, I gave him the lightest details—missing book, handed around all over the country, collector wants it back but isn't sure where it ended up, paper trail leading to the Roanokes. "What we need to do is talk to the

Roanokes and find out if they still have the book. All I need to do is confirm that I can turn it over to the client afterward."

"So we need to get you inside the ranch. Mano a mano, eh?"

"Something like that. Just a conversation."

"You don't just turn up on the Roanokes' doorstep, Mike."

"Well, this is why I'm talking to you, Bob. You've got the local knowledge. How do we get in to talk to them?"

"Heh. That's the one Regis used to ask for the million-dollar prize."

"Just the conversation. Not trying to deliver legal documents on them. It's a five-minute thing. How do we get in the door?"

"The Roanokes . . . They're not big on people, Mike. Especially since the whole politics thing blew up in their faces."

"Yeah," Trix said. "I was wondering about that."

"The Roanokes don't understand why they're not the Bushes, is the short version. They're old oil money, older than the Bushes. Old Man Roanoke spent some time in Joint Special Operations, deep spook stuff, has all kinds of weird friends. They figured they could jump right over building a power base in local politics and go right for the brass ring. The Old Man took a shot at kingmaking in the eighties, and that went wrong, so all his hopes were pinned on Junior.

"But what you need to get, Mike, is that the Roanokes are not normal. I mean, this isn't just 'the very rich are not like you and me.' There are stories."

"Uh-huh." I busied myself with beer.

"What kind of stories?"

"Oh, you just *had* to, didn't you, Trix?"

"I want to know. I couldn't just leave that hanging in the air."

Bob snorted.

"What's so funny about that?"

"Well, one story says that's how the Old Man was conceived. See, when guys are hanged by the neck, when their neck breaks they usually ejaculate. And apparently when the Old Man's pop hanged himself, his mom scraped up his spooge and, well . . . shoved it up herself. So, you know, 'hanging' . . . it just made me laugh, I'm sorry."

There was a clanking of cutlery on ceramics. The middle-aged couple sitting next to us had stopped eating, and were looking at Bob like they wanted to unload six-shooters in his face.

"See?" Bob rasped, leaning over the table. "They've got friends fucking *everywhere*."

The doors to the kitchen banged open. The waitress

emerged behind a long steel trolley, which she pushed with much pantomimed effort toward our table.

On it was a horizontal section of a bull. As if someone had taken a steer, chainsawed the sides off, and chucked the middle part on an eight-foot-long steel platter on wheels.

It still had a horn sticking out of it.

It was served blue; cold, basically, just seared to seal it and slapped on the plate. If it had still had both sides, a good vet could've gotten it up on its feet in an hour or so.

The waitress parked it at the end of the table, and gave Bob outsized, sawtoothed cutlery. "Message from chef," she growled. "He said to tell you that if you don't eat it all—again—he's going to take you outside and kick your nuts up into your lungs."

Bob laughed nervously. "What does he mean, again? I was sick last time. And the time before that, I ate it all, and neither you nor he were working that night. I ordered the Special, I'll eat the Special. Get me some steak sauce."

Trix and I must've been staring. Bob looked at us as he sawed off a chunk of microcooked steer and forked it onto his plate. It oozed clotted blood from the thick veins sticking out of the meat. "This is real Texas food," Bob said. "This is what we eat. Great fucking country, Texas."

I thought Bob was going to start crying again as he chewed the raw meat.

"Delicious," he mewled.

We sat there for five, ten minutes, silently watching Bob painfully shovel raw beef into his big, crushed face. Thankfully, our own food arrived at that point. A pound of meat on a flowery plate for Trix, and a huge chunk of rump for me. I turned it over with my fork. The skin was still on it. The skin's brand was still intact. A big *R*.

"Your fries," the waitress announced. A metal pail of fries with what looked like a gallon of melted cheese poured on top.

"I asked for the small portion," Trix said.

"That *is* the small portion," the waitress said.

Trix gave me a little smile. "I guess I know how they justify serving fries in a place that only serves stuff that came out of a cow."

"You got to eat it all," Bob muttered stickily. "It'll look bad for me otherwise."

Trix gave him her sweetest look. "Bob, I like you. I'm trying to make you feel comfortable. But, honestly, if you think I'm going to eat all this shit, you can just suck out my farts, okay?"

The middle-aged couple got up to leave. Bob choked back a sob and went back to his hideous dinner.

Trix met my eyes. "What? I'm only human, Mike.

117

Though I might not stay that way if I eat all this. They'll be pulling cholesterol out of my veins with a bulldozer."

"Quit moaning. My dinner's still got the skin on it."

"You're kidding me."

I lifted up one cheek of my pan-fried ass to show her the brand.

"*R*?"

"Roanoke." Bob coughed. "They're in the cattle business, too. It's a sign. Oh my God. Oh my God."

He forked another squirting chunk of beef into his mouth, looked up at the ceiling fan, and started yelling as he chewed. "Look! I'm eating it, you bastards! I'm eating it all!"

Bits of meat flew out of his mouth, hit the fan, and were evenly distributed all over the restaurant.

Chapter 25

Bob ate the entire damn thing, but was paralyzed afterward. After some cajoling, we arranged to briefly borrow a wheeled office chair from the restaurant's back room, and trundled him out to the parking lot in it. He was still sucking scraps of flesh off the horn, and bellowing that he'd showed them, he'd showed them all. Oh, and that the chef was a whore.

"Fuck this," I said. "Get the keys from him. I'll drive. We'll dump his crazy ass in front of the hotel and pay someone to move him or kill him or something."

"This is how you treat your friends?"

"He's a nutbag, Trix. Look at him. "

"Whooooores," said Bob.

"There you go. Get the fucking keys."

Trix patted him down and found the keys in his inside jacket pocket. "Thank God," she groaned. "I wasn't up for checking his pants."

Bob studied her with one eye, oddly drunken. "Mike never had the pretty girls before. How does he get the pretty girls now? I'm a goddamn *Texan*."

"You always talk to your buddies' girls like that?" she frowned, tossing me the keys.

I nearly dropped them.

"That's how I get into trouble." Bob teared up. "I'm so lonely." And, just at the point where we softened, he added, "Whooooores."

I opened up the rear door and tipped him into it.

"What about the chair?"

"Leave it here. They called that rump well done? If I'd poured my beer on it to wake it up it could've skated its way home in that damn chair. Get in."

"Oooh. Masterful."

"I'll spank you right here in the parking lot."

"Promises."

"Just get in the car."

As we pulled out of the parking lot, Bob seemed to pull out of his meat fugue a little. "Left at the lights. Something I want to show you."

"Whores?"

"No. Roanoke."

I looked for Trix's take. She shrugged. "It's what we came for. "

I took us left at the lights, and a handful more directions took us out of town. The dark came in hard. Trix looked up out of the window. "Stars," she said. "You don't see so many in New York. You don't realize."

"Kill the lights," said Bob, "and pull over here." We did, by a low wooden fence.

"Get out and look into the field."

"What are we looking for, Bob?"

"You'll see."

The night air was warm. The fence surrounded a large field littered with sleeping cattle. We wandered to the fence, put our feet on it, and waited.

"You look tense," Trix said. "Have a cigarette while we're waiting for whatever we're waiting for."

"The lighter flame will screw up my night vision."

"Huh," she said, thoughtfully. "You're a real detective, aren't you?"

"What did you think I was?"

"A cute, crazy guy who just fell into a crappy job. I don't think it ever occurred to me that you were, you know, a real detective. Knowing about things like night vision sounds like real detective stuff."

"Well, at least I'm still cute."

"I like funny-looking guys."

"Oh, thanks."

She giggled and hugged my arm. "You are just too easy to tease. Look. The cattle are waking up."

They were. And starting to move. Scattering. There was motion in the middle of the herd. Something running. I squinted, leaning in.

There was a naked man among the cattle. Silver hair in the starlight. Deep lines in his face when he moved out of the shadows of cows. Thin and leanly muscled, he sprinted between the frightened cattle, zigzagging wildly.

He stopped sharply as one cow moved diagonally in front of him. And then sprang like a jungle cat, landing on top of the beast. There was something in his hand that sparkled in the starlight. Wire. He drew it between his fists and made a looping motion under the cow's throat.

The naked old man garroted the cow with great industry, bringing it down. Hard muscles in his upper arms worked under gray skin. The cow twitched, shat itself, and died.

The old man clambered over the carcass and began to suckle at the dead beast's udders. Then crouched, face shiny with corpse-milk under the stars, threw his head back and howled like a wolf into the night.

We silently returned to Bob.

"That's Old Man Roanoke taking his nightly exercise," Bob whispered. "G. Gordon Liddy gave him that garrote."

Chapter 26

We drove back to the hotel in silence. Bob said he felt well enough to drive, so we stood there as he jammed himself back behind the wheel of the car and took off. We watched his car fishtail down the street and, a block and a half down, bury its front end in the door of a sports bar. Bob slumped out of the car door onto the street like a harpooned whale as the engine caught fire. Many large men came out of the bar with a surprising array of impromptu weaponry in hand.

"Fuck it," I said, and went inside.

"I'm going to stay here a minute," said Trix.

"You want to help him?"

"No, I want to see what they do to him. I'll be up in a minute."

There was someone waiting for me in the hotel room.

"So you think the Roanokes have it?" the White House chief of staff said, tying off in the armchair in front of an evangelist channel on the TV.

"Oh, God."

"That's good, Mr. McGill. Very good. We didn't know that. As you're probably aware, my president can't run for office again, unless we. Ha ha. Unless we change the Constitution. Can you imagine if Junior Roanoke had gotten to Washington? If he'd filled a room with the lawmakers, the great and the good, stood there at his lectern, opened the book and slammed it down? The Founders didn't imagine a time of radio and television. Politics was done in real time, with physical crowds. Just showing the people the pages on television, or reading them on radio, won't work. People have to be in the presence of the book, for its acoustic effect to work. If he'd ever been able to address serious audiences, the outcome would have been terrible. I don't think the Roanokes fully understand what they have."

I flopped into a chair. "What do you want?"

"I've gotten you an appointment with the Roanoke family for tomorrow morning at eleven. If they have the book, you're empowered to make them an offer of ten million dollars for it, contingent upon their permanent silence concerning its existence."

"I see."

"If they refuse, you're to use your cell phone to call 555 555-5555. Let it ring twice, and hang up."

"That's not a real number. 555 is the fake area code Hollywood movies use."

"We gave it to them. It works for us. Ring twice, then hang up."

"What happens then?"

"A fuel-air bomb of some description, I believe," he said, injecting himself with something brown and lumpy. "It'll look like the gasoline reservoir under their ranch went up, they tell me. Eleven o'clock, then. Good hunting, Mr. McGill."

He stood up to leave, shakily. "Oh, and don't worry, I haven't taken heroin in your hotel room. I have a cage of genetically modified green monkeys that express anti-cancer pharmaceuticals in their feces. Once a day, I have to inject dilute monkey turds. But it's better than dying, yes?"

"I'd have to think about that."

"Mmm. I imagine you would."

At the door, he stopped again.

"One more thing, Mr. McGill. The girl."

"Is none of your business. You're just the client. You don't get a say in how I do my job or who I spend time with."

"Aren't we scrappy these days, Mr. McGill?"

"I've not been in the best mood lately, for some reason."

"You don't enjoy your work, Mike. It is very sad. The girl, Mike, is a crazed omnisexual vaginalist with a string of lovers from genders they don't even have names for yet. She'll break your heart, Mike. Take my advice. Get your own room, put your pants on backward, and wear boxing gloves. It's good for you. Trust me. I'm the White House chief of staff."

He drifted out the door like a handful of black feathers cast on a winter's breeze.

Chapter 27

Trix came in. "I got the concierge to call the police. But the police beat Bob up, too."

I was drinking. I have two drinking faces, I've been told. The Social Drinking face, and the I Need to Drink Until the Front of My Brain Dies face.

"What's wrong?"

"We have an appointment with the Roanokes tomorrow at eleven."

"How did that happen?"

"My client was here. He told me things."

"He arranged it? Jesus."

"Yeah."

"You okay?"

I summoned a smile from somewhere. "Sure."

"You want to come to bed?"

No. I wanted to get really fucking drunk and then stab myself repeatedly.

"Nah. We're out of condoms. Forgot to buy any."

She sat on the arm of my chair. "What makes you think we need any?"

"Not without condoms, Trix."

"True. I don't know where you've been. But not what I meant." She rubbed her palm over the back of my hand. "I have hands. You have hands. You and me: it doesn't always have to be about vanilla humping, Mike."

"I like vanilla humping."

"Come here. I'm going to rewire your vanilla little brain with my bare hands."

Chapter 28

In the middle of the night, I said, "You said you were my girl. To Bob. You said he shouldn't talk like that to his buddies' girls."

"I did."

"Are you my girl?"

"Do you want me to be?"

"Do you want to be?"

"Why would you want me to be your girl?"

"Because you're smarter than I am. Because you see things I don't. Because you make me feel good just by looking at me. Because you fit right in my arms."

"Are you going to start singing?"

"And because sometimes I want to strangle you."

"That can be hot."

"I'm going to strangle you right now."

"You can't lift your arms."

". . . shit."

"I've never been monogamous in my life, Mike."

"I know."

"I can't do it."

"I'm not asking you to."

"But you want me to be your girl."

"If you want to be."

"I like girls, too."

"I don't want to watch or anything."

"I thought two girls was every man's dream."

"You're my dream."

"I don't believe you said that."

"I'm never going to admit I did, so get over it."

She laughed, low in her throat.

"How's this going to work, Mike?"

"There's only one thing I want. For as long as we last. Because I'm a depressing realist."

She tensed against me a little. "And what's that?"

"Other guys, I'm always going to have a problem with."

"That could be a problem."

"Yeah. And I'll cross that bridge when I come to it. But the only thing I really want?"

"Yeah?"

"No matter what you do? Come home with me at the end of the night."

And then she kissed me.

Chapter 29

If they don't give us the book they're going to *blow up the ranch*?"

"Still want to come?"

Okay, so maybe telling her that was a mistake. I'd arranged for a chauffeured car to take me to and from the Roanoke ranch outside town, and had suggested to Trix that maybe she wanted to stay at the hotel while I worked.

"Yes I do! I'm not letting you go into that on your own!"

"Are you serious?"

"Of *course* I'm serious! Jesus! They want to blow the place up if the Roanokes don't hand over the book? Wouldn't that blow up the book, too?"

"I'm figuring they worked that out and that they know something we don't. Maybe it's in a vault or something. Anyway, I don't think this counts as adventure."

She grabbed me by the back of the hair as I tried to put my pants on.

"I'm coming."

"Yes yes okay fuck ow okay yes."

"Good." She went off to find her boots, muttering.

Came back. "Mike. They wouldn't *really* . . ."

"The guy sat in that chair and injected monkey shit into his arm, Trix."

"Yeah. Getting boots now."

I counted off five seconds.

"He did *what*?"

"Don't be judgmental, Trix."

Chapter 30

It was a long drive out under an unforgiving sun. Even with the A/C cranked up in the rear of the car, I was regretting putting on the jacket and tie.

Trix was in boots, a short skirt, and a vest-top, showing off both sleeves of tattoos. "You think I'm covering up for the fucking Roanokes? I'm going to take a dump in their oven."

"Hell, I don't care. I need to look professional, you can look any way you like."

"I like you in suits. You should get a new one, though. That one's a bit frayed."

"Oh, that's not wear and tear. That's where the rat would eat at it."

"The rat."

"The super-rat in my office. One time I put tinfoil on

the floor outside his rat hole and hooked it up to a car battery. When he walked out on it, he should've lit up like a murderer on Old Sparky. But he stood up on his hind legs like Tony Montana in *Scarface*, you know? 'I can take your fucking bullets.' Soaked up every volt in the battery, jumped up on my desk and had sex with my sandwich until it dissolved. I hate that rat."

"Sometimes I wonder how close to hospitalization or suicide you really were before I met you."

"Three . . . maybe four hours."

The Roanoke ranch came into view. It gleamed under the sun. The whole complex was painted a brilliant bone white. As we pulled into the driveway, I noticed half of a cow's skeleton poking out of the lawn, jutting the way you see them sticking out of desert sand in Westerns.

A little farther down, there was a human skeleton sticking out of the ground in the same way. With a buzzard perched on it.

As we drove past, I craned to get a better look. The skeleton had been painted white. It could well have been fake. The buzzard, however, was real, and had had its feet wired onto one of the ribs. It had long since given up on escape, and just sat there with its head hanging like a depressed child's.

"You see what kind of people they are?" Trix said. "I'm going to flay this guy. You do your job, I'm not going to get in the way of that. But I'm going to just demolish this guy. It's like being driven into Hell knowing you can totally beat Satan's ass."

It took ten minutes to traverse the driveway into the ranch's courtyard. It was weirdly silent. As we got out of the car, a tall guy who reeked of bodyguard came out of the main house, looked around very professionally, and walked quickly toward us.

He put out his hand. "I'm John Menlove, head of security for the Roanoke family. You're Michael McGill and assistant, correct?" He put just enough force into the wide, careful handshake to measure my strength. I gave him about half a pound less pressure than I had, on reflex. I don't care if you're shaking over a contract, shaking with a bar drunk or shaking hands with your grandpa—you never, ever let someone know how strong you are.

"Please come inside. We have a security procedure to complete before I can introduce you to Mr. Roanoke. He's extremely protective of his family's safety, as I'm sure you can understand."

We were taken out of the sun into the main residence's cavernous, galleried hallway. A female security agent was produced, and she and Menlove patted Trix and me down, ran fingers through our hair, and requested to see our teeth. Trix was looking around the place as best she could, rolling her eyes from side to side—and then coughed out, "Holy *shit!*"

"What?"

"Please regulate your language in here, ma'am," the female security agent said.

"Eat me. Mike, look at the goddamn galleries!"

Running alongside the staircase, and across the landing gallery, was a long row of mounted, stuffed animal heads. Nothing special, you see that a lot—I don't want to sound jaded, but Old Rich Guys all went to the same fucking interior decorator or something—and my eyes just skipped over them. "What about them?"

Trix grabbed my head and turned it in the direction of that which was vexing her most. "There. Look."

". . . well, that can't be real."

"Mike, the guy has a dolphin head stuffed and mounted on his wall."

"There's no way that's real."

"Mike, this bastard cut Flipper's head off and put it on the wall."

"Maybe Flipper had it coming."

"Mike."

"How the hell do you remember Flipper, anyway? Flipper was caught in a tuna net before you were born."

"I saw reruns as a kid. And you take that back about the tuna net. *Look* up there. My God, I think that's a kitten head next to it."

Menlove was looking uncomfortable. "Perhaps we can go through to the living room."

"No, no, give us a minute here. I know that's a moose, but, next to it there . . . would you know if that's a white tiger?"

"It might be. Mr. Roanoke will be free to speak to you in just a few moments."

"And that there. That's a seal, isn't it?"

"Oh my God, Mike. Roanoke has a seal head on his wall."

In fact, the longer we looked, the more animals we identified, and none of them really belonged on a polished wooden base and hanging on a wall. Even the moose. Because it turned out it was a reindeer. And someone had applied rouge to its nose.

"Yes. That was me. My daughter was naughty. I told her that I had killed Rudolph and mounted him in my gallery, and so there would be no Christmas."

Old Man Roanoke, tall and lean and lined and surprisingly easy to recognize with all his clothes on. Flanked on one side by a security agent, and on the other by a male nurse. He was in blue jeans and a work shirt, which is another weird quirk of Rich Old Men. Just one of the guys here. Blue jeans and a work shirt, salt of the earth, working man like yourself. Like they're somehow uncomfortable about being rich enough to sleep in a bed made of vaginas being pulled around the town at night by a fleet of gold-covered midgets.

I don't go into situations like this in the best of moods in any case. But I found myself becoming unusually irritated. Trix, God help her, was practically vibrating with rage just simply by being there.

The male nurse cleared his throat. "I'm uncomfortable with this interview at this time of the day. So, please, let's get on with it. Mr. Roanoke is in something of a delicate medical balance."

I raised an eyebrow. "You're ill?"

He grinned the way lizards should grin; slow and lazy, like a lizard early on a cold morning. "I have Roanoke's Disease."

"You'd think you would have seen that coming," Trix said.

Roanoke scanned Trix quickly and then shot Menlove a filthy look. "There's a girl in here, Mr. Menlove."

"We've checked her out, sir. She actually has a very small penis. Like a baby boy's. Undescended testes."

"Okay. Good. Like your agent there. Seems to be an

awful lot of that about. Must be the water the poor people have to drink. They do drink water, don't they?"

Menlove straightened, moved behind me. "I hear they can't afford water, sir, and drink something called Mountain Dew." Leaned in and hissed in my ear, "Just roll with it, please. This is my life. This is how I have to live. Help me out."

I stepped to Trix, gave her hand a quick sharp squeeze. She flicked her eyes to mine, read me, and shrugged.

"Ah," Roanoke said. "You would be McGill. Would you like to see my garrote, McGill?"

I decided not to mention that I'd already seen it in action. "I'm really just here to discuss a rare book that your family purchased a few years ago from a police officer in Ohio."

He pulled the garrote out of his pants pocket. "This garrote," he said, dangling it in front of his eyes like a stage hypnotist's watch, "was fashioned from the guts of Sand Gooks."

"Sand Gooks."

"Oh yes. They hunt me. I have fought the Sand Gook for thirty years or more. They know my name. Their men are impotent with hate and their women smell like a baby's graveyard."

"Mr. Roanoke really should be in bed," the male nurse said.

"I need that book."

"Yes," Roanoke croaked. "I know who you work for. Menlove! Did you check under their car?"

"I ran the broom under it and everything."

"Good. The Sand Gook can cling to the chassis of a car and draw sustenance from the tailpipe. I know who you work for. They give succor to the Sand Gook."

Trix couldn't let that one slide. "You know, not only is that term totally offensive, but the current government is prosecuting a war in the Middle East that uses torture in the pursuit of securing oil interests just like yours."

"You, sir, are a fool," he told her. "Which is perhaps only to be expected from a man in a skirt. Their 'war' is a girl's war. It has nothing to do with oil. It has everything to do with the awful preterhuman aspect of the Sand Gook. We cannot allow people who can become invisible to share a planet with us."

Trix turned wide eyes to me. "Okay. I officially give up. Go to it."

"Mr. Roanoke. You know who I work for. You understand that there will be repercussions if this interview is unsatisfactory. I'm empowered to offer you a significant sum in exchange for the book. Please. Let us get to business now."

"That damn book. We could have had *control*, if we'd used that book. The Middle East would be glass and I wouldn't be negotiating with damn Russians to buy missiles to protect my property. But the boy wouldn't use it. Promise me something, Mr. McGill. If you ever meet a real woman, instead of cavorting with tattooed hermaphrodites, keep a stone in your pocket."

I just had to. "A stone?"

"Yes. For killing a retarded child when your woman squats it out into the world. The skulls are soft. It's like punching calf's liver. I lost my stone. And so I have my children. I should have found a less defective wife. My sperm festered in her womb. I may as well have masturbated into a garbage can. Can you smell that?"

"Smell what?"

Roanoke was sniffing the air hard. The male nurse started rummaging in the zippered pouch on his hip, which rattled with pills and metal. "Mr. Roanoke occasionally suffers olfactory hallucinations. I did mention that this wasn't a good time."

Roanoke abruptly dropped to all fours. No one seemed to know how to handle this.

On his hands and knees, he pawed over the polished wooden floor to my crotch, which he sniffed like a dog.

"You," he snarled, "have known the dusky terrorist pleasure of a Sand Gook woman."

Only four times in my life has my hand literally itched to have a gun in it. This was number five.

"What was it like?" the old man asked, unzipping his jeans. "Was it good?" He pushed his gnarled hand inside his pants.

"Okay. That's it," said the male nurse.

"No," he howled. "I need to know." His hand was working.

The male nurse withdrew a hypodermic syringe from the hip bag, bit off its plastic lid, and jammed it into Roanoke's neck. He flipped over in some kind of reaction seizure, brownish urine spraying from within his twitching fist.

"Thank Christ for that," sighed Menlove, visibly unclenching. "Get him into bed. Mr. McGill, I'm sorry about this."

"Not as sorry as I am. Wake him up."

The male nurse snorted. "He's not going to wake up for a few hours."

"He's going to wake up now."

"Look, you're not going to get your book," Menlove said. "Leave it."

"Let me put it this way. If I don't get my book, there's a chance that something seriously antithetical to your current state of health could happen in the next little while."

". . . what's my current state of health?"

"Alive."

His eyes narrowed.

"I'm not threatening you. What's going on here is a little bigger than that, and I'm not entirely in control of it. I need him awake."

Trix kicked the old man in the stomach. He just kind of puffed out some air. Trix kicked him a few more times.

"He's not waking up, Trix."

"Oh, I'm past that and into pure entertainment value now," she said, prodding at his nose with the point of her boot. "What're you going to do?"

I fished out my cigarettes. "I don't know. I mean, he wants me to make the call if I don't get the book. I can wait for him to call me, but I can't tell him I have the book, because I can't produce it. Which brings us back to square one. If the Roanokes don't give up the book . . ."

"What happens, Mr. McGill?" Menlove asked, slipping his hand inside his jacket.

"People I don't know and have no control over will do something extraordinarily horrible to this ranch and will never ever be prosecuted for it," I told him.

". . . you're not telling me he was right about the Sand Gooks, are you?"

I lit up, watching his face work. "How long have you been working here?"

"Eight years. I wake up with a gun in my mouth every morning."

"Yeah, well, you might want to think about doing that right now. If the old man's out for the count—"

"He pass out again?" came a big, twanging voice. A man in his early fifties, short and trim in tennis whites, bounded into the hall from a rear entrance. "He didn't do that thing with his pants first, did he? I'm real sorry if he did. I'm Jeff Roanoke Jr. Anything I can help you folks with?"

He flipped his tennis racquet from right to left so he could shake hands with me, a wide soft grip. His eyes locked on to mine for a couple of seconds, judging. He wasn't stupid. He was letting me think I was stronger than him, and checking my reaction.

"Mike McGill. Good to meet you. I'm here on behalf of a client about a rare book we believe entered your possession a few years ago, purchased from a police officer in Ohio . . . ?"

Roanoke's oddly boyish, rubbery face stretched into an easy grin. "That old thing?"

"I'm empowered to offer you a significant sum to obtain it."

"Well, hell, son, we should go to my den and talk about it. C'mon back."

He stopped, on one foot, and looked back over his shoulder. "No girls."

Trix rolled her eyes. "I'll be in the car. With the engine running, Mike."

Chapter 31

Down two flights of stairs, through some heavy doors, into a bare concrete corridor lit by caged lamps hung from the walls, to a steel hatch that Junior spun the wheel of with practiced ease.

"This is the den?"

"Daddy doesn't like it when I call it the bunker. Bad associations with the past, he says. So, well, whatever keeps the old man happy."

Inside was a dark, warm space from the 1950s. Baseball pennants pinned to rich wood-paneled walls, old globes and maps, Tiffany lamps, an antique radio, and a bar straight out of a Rat Pack musical.

"Drink?" Junior said, walking over to the big mahogany desk at the far side of the room.

"No, thanks. I'd like to get straight down to business, if I could."

"Businessman? That's good. What's your business, Mike?"

"A book you possess. A, um, an alternate Constitution of the United States."

Behind the desk, he was opening its deep central drawer. "Ah," he said, with rueful knowledge. "That old thing."

"I represent someone who wants that book very badly. I'm empowered to offer you ten million dollars for it. But the deal has to be struck today."

His eyes widened and his mouth shrank. "Today?"

"Yes, sir. This is a matter of the utmost urgency to my client."

"That damned book." He sat down heavily in the big leather chair behind the desk. "I tried reading it once. It was the strangest thing. I dropped it down on the desk, right here, to read it, and it was like my goddamn eyeballs were bugging out. I didn't understand a word of the text but I couldn't stop reading it. And Daddy wanted me to use that damned thing . . ." He trailed off, looking down into whatever was in the open drawer, out of my line of vision.

"With your father, um, out of commission, I was hoping you could help me."

"I wasn't ready to be president. I'm *going* to be. But I wasn't ready then. And I'm not ready for this today."

"No offense, Mr. Roanoke, but you need to be ready for this. This is extremely important."

"Gimme . . . gimme a second," he whispered. And withdrew an old gas mask, the full-face kind that has the airtank and compressor hanging from the thick pipe connected to the mouth of the mask. I noticed that the bottom of the tank had been sawed off, and stepped in to see what he was doing.

In the deep drawer was a small mountain of cocaine. The only thing it was missing were gulls nesting in the crevices. Tony goddamn Montana would have quailed at the sight of it.

Junior shoved the open end of the tank into the white pile and flipped on the compressor. Enough coke to kill a flock of young tyrannosaurs was sucked up into Junior's head. He ripped off the mask and shrieked. Bloody residue dripped out of the tank and back onto the pile. Eyes bulging, he looked down at the smashed heap of marching powder. "My God! I see Jesus! I see His Face in these Satanic drugs! I am Saved! Glory Be!"

He looked at my face and laughed. "Relax, sport. I'm just practicing. I'm going to be president one day. It's important to get these things right."

"The book—"

"Fuck the book. I've just had a religious conversion. Were you impressed?"

"I kind of expected you to be a religious man, in any case," I said, looking for something heavy.

"Ringo says religion is a political tool," he honked, squeezing his eyes shut and trying to claw through to his sinuses.

"Who's Ringo?"

Junior wrenched open the left-hand drawer in the desk and ripped from it a scrawny-looking cuddly toy with its eyes plucked out and awful stains on its mouth.

"*This* is Ringo!" he exulted. "*Ringo* is my *friend*!" He clutched the scabby thing to a chest already pebble-dashed with cocaine, bloodclots, and snot.

My back bumped into the door. "And . . . he says things, does he?"

"Yeahhhhhh," Junior sighed, stroking Ringo's stomach in a disturbingly sexual way.

"Okay. He speaks to you. That's fine. However, I'd appreciate it if you could save the conversation in your head for later and address the matter at hand."

"Ringo could speak to you, too."

"Yeah," I said. I gave a halfhearted wave in the direction of the stained object in Junior's fist. "Hi, Ringo."

"No," Junior intoned, unsmiling. "You have to press his stomach."

"Why?"

"You have to. You can't leave until you've pressed his stomach."

On reflection, I decided that this would be easier than, say, having warm salty water shot into my dadpaste factory. I could handle this. Junior was obviously a coke fiend and a congenital shitbrain. Why not humor him? It seemed to me to be the simplest path.

"I'd be happy to. But on the understanding that we start dealing like men after this, yes?"

Junior held the skinny mutilated horror out at arm's length toward me. "Press his fucking stomach!"

I moved forward and pushed two fingers into the thing's gut. A voicebox ground into life with a hideous low rasp. Like an eighty-year-old chainsmoking hooker who hadn't yet slipped in her teeth.

"Women are best when they can't talk any more," it said.

I flinched back, but Junior grabbed my wrist. Tendons stood out in his arm, and his knuckles whitened. He was using all his strength. And it wasn't all that.

"Morrrrre," he growled.

I pressed the stomach again.

"Where's my dinner, bitch?"

And:

"God says queers are special firewood."

"That's enough," I said.

"I said fucking *more*," Junior said.

I twisted my arm around and he squealed as his wrist bent, but he refused to let go. I put the base of my left hand into his nose and turned it into a bathmat.

He reeled backward, clutching the toy, his fingers twisted into it. It kept rasping: "Americans are born, not made." "Stupid people just like stuff simple." "If they can't see you drinking, you're not an alcoholic."

Junior dragged himself into the seat behind the desk. "You're doomed now, you stupid fuck. I'm gonna be the president one day. Daddy says. He says presidents are people like us."

Ringo said: "Fuck America and get rich like astronauts."

"Oh, God," Junior groaned. "Where's my Womb Thing?"

He scrabbled in the desk for a moment and produced a glass screw-top jar filled with a thick, clotted yellow fluid. Junior unzipped a badly discolored little penis and began to jerk off into the jar with the maniacal fury of an ugly ape in humping season.

I snatched up one of the big Tiffany lamps, flipped it around in my hand, and brought the edge of its heavy base down in his lap.

He screamed and jerked forward, inadvertently head-butting his desk.

I gave him a few minutes. In the course of my work, I've had occasion to hit people before. I can tell when I've hit them too hard, because they always puke. I can tell when they wake up, and I can tell when they're faking it. Junior woke up after a couple of minutes, but was playing dead.

I stepped over to his bar, unstopped a bottle of vodka, and poured it over his head. He was good, I'll give him that. Barely fluttered an eyelash.

Flicking my lighter, however, miraculously brought him back to life.

"Mr. Roanoke. I left my sense of humor in Columbus, Ohio. You and your father are shitbags of quite epic proportions. But I have no wish to see you dead. Unless I get that book now, the people whom you failed to remove from office will destroy this place, with you in it. I need the book now. Or else you will discover not only that you can live through having your head set on fire, but that death by bombing actually hurts more."

His eyes were very wide, and he wasn't blinking. "I don't have it."

I slapped him. "Why are you fucking with me?"

"I don't have it. I had to give it to someone. Daddy doesn't know."

"Bullshit."

"I made her sign a receipt. So she wouldn't . . . she knew things about me. I had to make her not talk. She said she had the video locked somewhere safe, and that someone would go and get it if she disappeared. And I didn't have any money."

"*You*? Didn't have any *money*?"

He looked sad. "Some things are very expensive."

"Show me the receipt."

"It's in the desk."

"If I think you're pulling anything but a piece of paper out of there, I'm going to ignite your head."

With my lighter held within his halo of vodka fumes, he slowly withdrew an envelope. It looked like he'd been doodling on the back of it at some point. On closer inspection, it appeared that he'd been practicing his alphabet.

I popped the envelope. The sheet of paper inside had been typed, thank God.

"You gave the book to a prostitute, didn't you?"

"Yes."

"Well, you'll be glad to know that there's apparently precedent for that. Last known address?"

"Right there. It checks out. My family has friends there who keep tabs on her for me."

I folded the paper, put it into my jacket, tossed the envelope at him. "I have to talk someone out of turning your house into Baghdad, now."

I got up and walked to the door. Behind me, a rasping voice said, "Break America's heart before it breaks yours." I didn't look back.

Chapter 32

True to her word, Trix was out in the car, and the engine was running. Since I was clearly not carrying a book, Trix was freaking out a little bit.

"Quit strolling and get in the fucking car!"

Two seconds after I got in, the car took off like a fighter plane. She'd obviously been talking to the driver, who was perspiring heavily.

"Mike, what happened? Are they going to do it?"

I took out my cell phone and dialed all those fives. Counted off two rings. And let it ring.

On the fifteenth ring, the chief of staff answered the phone. "I said two rings, McGill."

"They don't have the book." I was forcing myself to speak slowly. "I have in my possession a receipt for the book, which I believe to be genuine."

"Oh, you believe it, do you?"

"You hired me for my skills. Try listening."

". . . I think I liked you better before you started acting like you grew a pair, McGill."

"Jeff Roanoke Jr. gave the book to a prostitute in exchange for her continued silence regarding services rendered for what I presume was an extended period of time. He's also maintained enough sporadic surveillance on her to give a credible assurance that she remains in the location given on the receipt document. He was not in a position to lie convincingly to me."

"And why is that?"

"Because he was seriously confused by controlled substances. And because I was going to light his head on fire."

The chief of staff laughed over the phone. Wind passing through bones.

"Okay, Mike. Okay. What was your opinion of the Roanokes?"

"In my considered opinion, it would be far more cruel to let them live."

More laughter, and then he abruptly hung up.

I smiled at Trix. "Everyone's going to live."

She sagged in her seat. "Christ."

"It's not all good news," I said. "We have to go to Las Vegas now."

"Vegas? Vegas is cool. We could get married by Elvis."
She leaned over to tap the sweaty driver on the shoulder.
"Hey. Everything's okay. You can slow down now."

He threw up over the steering wheel.

Chapter 33

We got a late flight out to Vegas. Trix watched the night outrace us from her window seat and eventually fell asleep.

The business-class section was empty but for us and an older man sitting across the aisle from me. We nodded and smiled at each other a couple of times and, as the cabin crew left us for dead and Trix began a soft purring snore, he spoke to me.

"Long day, huh?" He smiled, indicating Trix.

"You could say that."

"Texas can hit you like that. But Vegas, my friend. You never want to sleep. Going for pleasure?"

"Business."

"Me, too, kinda. Business and pleasure all in one, you might say."

"You a gambler?"

His face was oddly stiff in places, heavily lined in others. His eyes looked a little stretched, at the sides. I figured him for about seventy, and a serious plastic surgery freak in earlier days. Your face doesn't just grow into that shape. He smiled, knowing I was checking him over, but the smile lines didn't travel up into his forehead. Botox.

"Cop?" he asked, mildly.

"Private detective." I sketched a grin for him. "Don't worry. Your secrets are safe with me."

"I hope so." He smiled. "I kill people, you know."

We laughed quietly. But after a while, I stopped laughing. And he was still laughing.

"God, I hate that term 'serial killer,' don't you? Something about it just makes me think of Flash Gordon or something. Old matinees."

"I never really thought about it," I said, checking to make sure I still had whiskey in my glass.

"Occupational hazard, I'm afraid," he sighed, leaning back in his chair. "You can't help but worry about the way you're represented. I'm thinking about suing someone."

"I imagine that'd be difficult." I had no doubt he was what he was telling me he was. This is my life, after all. But I couldn't help but be impressed with the way I was handling it. Small things bring joy, some days.

"Well, yeah," he said. "But, you know, when an actor or pop star has untruths published about them, they sue, and I kind of feel like I should have the same recourse. And justice for all, right?"

"But you kill people. Where's the justice there?"

"Oh, they had it coming. If people will dress like librarians and schoolgirls they should expect these things to happen. I don't see why they should be afforded extra protection for that kind of behavior. And in any case, two wrongs don't make a right. Slander is bad no matter who you're doing it to, surely?"

"Slander?"

"Let's get another drink," he said, pushing the service call button above his head. "You don't watch much TV, am I right?"

"Not really."

"I'll have a whiskey, and I believe so will my friend here. Doubles. Thank you. What was I saying? Yes. TV. Yet another documentary about me on TV the other week. One of these science channels. You'd expect intelligent coverage from a TV channel like that, wouldn't you? Of course you would. They got a good actor to do the voiceover narration, too. My age. Alan something. Used to be in that very black comedy show about the Korean War."

"Alan Alda?"

"Alan Alda! How he made me laugh in that show. And the women dressed well, too. Never enough blood, though. Which always made me a little sad. But I guess it was supposed to make you a little sad, wasn't it? That rueful smile? Very clever show. He narrated the documentary about me. I'm not blaming him, obviously. He didn't write it. One day I will meet the mediocrity that wrote that. I mean, do I look like the kind of man who has difficulty socializing?"

I had to be honest. "Actually, no."

"No. Of course not. I don't want to sound egotistical, but, really, do I look like someone who had problems meeting women? I've been married three times. And"—he leaned over the aisle and looked me right in the eye—"I only killed *two* of them."

"Huh."

"Yeah. How about that? They can stick that in their pipe and smoke it. So much for *America's Terror: The Mad Virgin.* I have four children. *Had* four children. Funny thing. I always thought it was a joke, about liking children but not being able to eat a whole one. But it's quite true."

I started stabbing my own call button.

"The Mad Virgin. My God. I could sue them, you know. Some of the others have been better, mind you. I collect them. Twelve documentaries about me. Three

Hollywood movies using aspects of my work. I sometimes hoped to be played one day by Sean Connery. But you just know he'll use his own accent. I think that'd spoil it for me."

"I can imagine."

"You have a very understanding way about you. I appreciate that. Cheers." He polished off a finger of whiskey. I tossed down about a hand's worth and resumed stabbing the service button.

"Yeah, thanks. Leave the bottle. My friend and I are very thirsty."

"Good man," he said, holding out his glass. "So. You and your lovely companion. What business do you have in Sin City?"

"Trawling through America's sick underbelly in search of people who are holding a book the White House wants back."

"Now, that sounds interesting. What kinds of things have you seen? This is such a wonderful, rich country. When you look under the covers it holds to its trembling little chin in the night."

So I told him.

He considered, and then said, "Is that all?"

"That's not enough?"

"Young man, I have to tell you: if you think that con-stitutes a trawl of America's true cultural underground, you may have a nasty shock in your future. Let me ask you a question. Our meeting, here, tonight: do you consider this perhaps a waypoint in your perceived descent into the muck of modern life?"

"Sure. You kill people for wearing crap clothes, from what I can make out. The only reason why you're not trying to fuck my girlfriend in the gall bladder with a screwdriver as she sleeps is because you can see her boobs and she's wearing makeup."

Yeah, I was pretty drunk. He took it pretty equably.

"Not as accurate a summation as you think, but, yes, I'll allow it. My point is that I'm not the underground. You think that drinking with a serial killer takes you into the midnight currents of the culture? I say bullshit. There's been twelve TV documentaries, three movies, and eight books about me. I'm more popular than any of these designed-by-pedophile pop moppets littering the music television and the gossip columns. I've killed more people than Paris Hilton has desemenated, I was famous before she was here and I'll be famous after she's gone. I am the mainstream. I am, in fact, the only true rock star of the modern age. Every newspaper in America never fails to report on my comeback tours, and I get excellent reviews."

"And what about . . . all the rest of it?"

"I think I've seen a lot of it on the Internet."

"I can't use the Internet. My ex sends me things. Photos."

"Perhaps I should send you some photos sometime. Consider this, though. If I've seen it on the Internet, is it still underground? 'Underground' always connoted something hidden, something difficult to see and find. Something underneath the surface of things, yes? But if it's on the Internet—and I do praise the Lord that I lived long enough to see such a wondrous thing—it cannot possibly be underground."

"People show pictures of their asses on the inner-web."

"Yes. And it's a wonderfully useful tool for stalking people. What's more, my personal fetish—and it is a fetish, I fully appreciate and understand that—requires trophies of a sort, and I find that storing them as images on private Web space does very nicely. I don't have to carry them with me, you see? Wherever there is an Internet connection, I can reach my collection. I mean, that's just marvelous. My point, however, is that the Internet is more than a system for holding pictures, whether it be of people's backsides or my hands all slick and yellow with human subcutaneous fat. It is the greatest mass-communication tool ever invented, and utterly democratic beyond the entry-level requirement of having a computer."

"Now holllld on. A seventy-year-old serial killer is gonna lecture me on the intynets."

"Seventy-one. And I think it's important you learn this, for the future of your enterprise. We agree that if something is available on television and in bookstores and the papers and all, it's mainstream, yes?"

"Sure."

"Well, then, how can something on the world's electronic mass-communication net not also be mainstream? It's easily found. You told me your friend there saw acquaintances of the gentlemen from Ohio on the Web."

"Did I? Okay. I'm a little drunk."

"There you are, you see? It's not that strange a world, when you can see images of men with testes full of saline just as easily as you can visit the wonderful world of Disney online. That's not underground. It's mainstream. Just like me."

I lifted my glass. "Y'know? S been a absolute pleasure speaking with you. A lot v things r mushmush clearer now."

He brought his glass to mine and we bumped plastic. "And you, young man, are on a great adventure, and I salute you."

We drank, and poured, and drank, and really it was very nice. Me and the serial killer.

Chapter 34

From a distance, the Strip looked like it was covered in a dozen different colors of blossom on a wet spring morning.

Up close, the blanket of petals turned out to be a thick coating of discarded handbills from pimps and porn operations, stuck to the road by rainfall.

Reduced to a pulpy sludge by dirty rain, they dulled the footfalls. We squelched our way through ANAL HOOKERS and PHONE DOMINATION under the ugly gray dawn light, walking from the street up to the hotel I'd found us.

Down from the pyramid of the Luxor, the European castles, and some wetbrain's idea of Paris, this was Vegas's newest development. Trix got a look at it and punched me in the arm.

The Freedom was a hotel within an outsize copy of the statue of Jesus that stands outside Rio de Janeiro in Brazil. Only in this version Jesus was dressed in an Uncle Sam suit.

"We're staying in the hat," I said, rubbing my arm.

"You're a pervert," she hissed.

"Oh, that's good coming from you."

She wrapped her arms around herself and stalked ahead of me.

"There will be no sex for you until we leave this place," she said.

I stood there alone in the eerily silent streets of Las Vegas and listened to my penis cry.

The ground floor was vast. You could have fit my entire street into the place. Bellhops with name badges bearing the title FREE MAN scuttled up to us and attempted to steal our luggage. The place looked still half-built, the massive American flags covering scaffolding and holes in dividing walls. We were checked in smoothly, but my attention was drawn to a collection of tents some three hundred yards across the floor.

"Refugees," the receptionist snarled. "They got off the boat in California and took a Greyhound straight here. Someone said they saw the hotel on TV and thought we wanted their tired and their hungry. Who knew other people even had TV?"

Trix leaned over the polished counter. "I want to kill you," she whispered.

I grabbed her arm and guided her away, sweeping the keycards off the counter as I went. She tried to shake me off, but I sank my fingers into her upper arm and marched her to the elevators.

"That hurts."

"Stop fucking around."

"I can't believe you brought me here."

"I thought it'd be funny."

"It turns my stomach."

"These people just work here. They didn't build it."

"Did you hear her?"

"So she's dumb. You want to kill people for being dumb?"

"Yes."

The elevator doors opened with a little Yankee Doodle Dandy chime. I put Trix inside it. Abraham Lincoln leered down at us from the ceiling.

"Look," I said. "You don't get to keep the parts of the country you like, ignore the rest, and call what you've got America. You didn't vote for the president, right?"

"Fuck no."

"No. I bet she did. Half the people in America did. More than half the people in America believe in God. You don't get to just ignore that. I know you like telling me about new stuff and showing me that there's a whole other society in America and all that shit. So now I'm showing you: this is what the rest of the people have, okay?"

She looked up at Abe and shuddered. "This is horrible, Mike."

"If I coped with having a bucket of salty water injected into my balls, you can cope with this."

"You're teaching me a lesson. Jesus."

"Actually, I just thought it'd be funny. The lesson just came to me a minute ago. And don't blaspheme. You're riding an elevator up to Jesus' hat."

"I'm going to be sick."

"Have you got 666 tattooed on you someplace?"

"You may never get a chance to look for it again, Michael McGill."

There was a plaster bas-relief of Jesus on the wall over the bed. The bed had a wooden slat down the middle that divided it in half. And the toilet played "Onward Christian Soldiers" when you lifted the lid.

"I think I can feel blisters forming on my brain," said Trix, balled up and rocking slowly in the corner.

Chapter 35

I went back down to the front desk, bought a map, and arranged a car hire. I returned to the sound of Trix giggling.

"I found this in a drawer," she said. She was waving around a piece of pink plastic that looked like a smaller version of one of those old-fashioned lemon-squeezing spikes, the kind you ream out the flesh of the fruit with. She flipped it around in her hand to show me the handle. The handle was a molded representation of a little baby with a halo.

"It's a Baby Jesus buttplug," she squealed.

"You're kidding me."

"It gets better." She laughed. She opened a drawer in the room's desk, and produced a wrapped condom from a small box therein. She unwrapped it, grinning. "Look," she said, as it unfurled.

The reservoir tip had Jesus' face on it.

"Oh, God," I said.

"Exactly! This drawer is full of Christian sex resources! I take back everything I said. I love it here."

"Trix, I'm not exactly a churchgoing man, but there's no way in Hell I'm going to ejaculate into Jesus' head."

"Oh, we'll see about that."

"Nor am I going to wear the little baby Jesus in my ass."

"Spoilsport."

Chapter 36

As the sun went down, we left the hotel and walked a while on the Strip. Dancing fountains and robot pirates for an hour, among the tourists and the beaten-looking locals and the pimps and losers handing out cards and flyers for sex and porn.

No one in Vegas ever looks like they're having fun.

An old colleague of mine from there once told me of his plan to return to Vegas and get rich. He was going to install slot-machine public toilets on the Strip. You'd have to put a coin in the slot and pull the lever to get into the toilet. And if the reels were not your friend? The door would stay locked. He envisioned great long lines of people dying for a piss and throwing handfuls of metal into the machine for the chance of taking a leak before their bladders exploded.

He works in advertising now.

We spent a while in a bar with the map—no escape from the ringing cacophony of the machines—and then headed back to the Freedom to pick up the car, a two-seater new-style MG that I liked the sound of. It was small and sharp, great for navigating through the Strip. Once we were off the Strip, though, parking-lot country unfolded before us, as far as the eye could see. We could have been back in Columbus, San Antone, or any other city.

It was dark when we found the address. A cheap-as-dirt area, a bungalow that was ten years old but looked ready to fall apart like a stack of cardboard in the rain. The lights were all on, and there were a bunch of cars parked around it, but it was weirdly quiet. It immediately felt wrong.

"I kind of wish I had a gun," I said quietly.

"Why?" I made her nervous. Which was good.

"Something doesn't ring right. I don't know what. If I tell you to run, head straight back to the car, no argument. Okay?"

"Okay."

We got out of the car. Something was bugging me. And I was also disturbed by wanting a gun twice in as many days.

It was getting darker.

There were voices behind the door, low and fast. I rang the door buzzer a couple of times. No one came out. I leaned on it.

A tall, florid-faced Latina with purple streaks in her hair and mascara streaks on her face ripped the door open.

"Are you the paramedics?" she shrieked.

"No. We're here to see Alexis Perez."

She went to slam the door. I put my foot in it.

"It's very important."

"No it's not. She can't see you."

"Why not?"

She lost it. "Because I think she's dying!"

I straight-armed the door open, knocking the woman down, and boiled through into the house. I just had to follow the voices.

There were four other Latinas in the kitchen and one on the floor, naked but for a bra, laying on her front and shaking violently. There were livid red pinholes on her backside. The four standing may as well have been laying down for all the use they were. They were terrified.

I shoved one out of the way, went down on one knee, and pushed the girl over into recovery position. There was foam on her lips and her eyes were rolling back into her head. She was making long, drawn-out creaking noises, her chest convulsing.

I looked up at them. "Who dialed 911?"

The one I knocked down stamped back into the room, big hands balled into fists. "I did, bitch."

"Call them again. Her lungs are locking up. Anyone know if she has asthma or allergies?"

They shook their heads dumbly.

"Do any of *you* use inhalers?" Nothing. I rolled her all the way over into shock position, ripping off my jacket and balling it up to put under her feet.

It was then that I noticed she was a he.

Trix was at the kitchen sink. Anger shook in her voice. She said, "Who brought this shit in here?"

I got the jacket under the ladyboy's feet and straightened up. There were large-bore needles in the sink, and canisters of something that looked like they belonged on a hardware store's shelf.

Trix turned on them. "Come on. Which of you *retards* brought this shit in here and shot her up with it?"

"What's going on, Trix?"

"It's a pumping party, Mike. It's a party where male-to-female transgendered people with *acute fucking body dysmorphia who can't fucking read*"—she spat that into the face of the one who answered the door—"inject themselves with silicone to give themselves a more womanly shape."

"Hey, look, she wanted it," Purple-streaks said.

Trix slapped her, hard. "It's *industrial-grade* silicone, you stupid fucking asshole! It's caulk! It's sealant! This is the shit you *waterproof bathtubs* with! They lubricate shit on *oil rigs* with this stuff!"

I looked down at the boy fighting for breath. "Oh my God."

"Yeah," Trix said. "It's not sterile, it can come mixed with paraffin, and it can kill you in like half a dozen ways. It came up in a transgendered activism workshop I sat in on last summer. Pumping parties. Boys in dresses who want J-Lo's butt."

"What can we do?"

"She's in toxic shock. And from the sound of her breathing, I bet you the stuff is migrating up into her lungs. It goes everywhere. How much," she rounded on Purple-streaks again, "did you shoot into her?"

"Tonight, or in total?"

Trix got in her face. "He's got a gun and I can own you with my bare fucking hands! How *much*?"

"Two thousand CCs each buttock. That was just tonight."

The boy on the floor stopped breathing.

Trix and I both applied CPR, but it was no good. The

lungs were full of industrial sealant. By the time the paramedics arrived, it was all over.

The one with the purple streaks sat on the floor by the sink, knees drawn up, saying nothing but "Oh, God, Alexis," over and over again.

But Alexis was dead.

Chapter 37

Trix and I gave the cops an edited version of our reason for being there. The attending officers from homicide were a couple of old bulls of the type that I'm always comfortable dealing with. Macabre as it may have seemed, I needed to get a look around the house, and I laid it out for them.

We got to talking, and they in turn laid things out for us.

They knew Alexis was a hooker. His/her pimp was well known to them. Tim Cardinal, Teflon Tim, from whom all useful charges slid. He was a common-or-garden pimp with extraordinary luck. You get old bulls like these two talking about the ones who got away and it's like asking your grandfather about the war. Trix and I were lucky we had nowhere to be.

After a while, and the potted history of Teflon Tim and

the five murders he'd wriggled out of, the pair agreed that we could do a quick sweep of the house for the book. The case was as clear-cut as it got, we weren't going to mess with the investigation, and they got a favor in New York City owed them in the future. Connections and under-the-desk favors count for a lot.

Alexis didn't have a lot of stuff, and it was a small place. After an hour, we were certain that the book wasn't there.

"This thing's valuable, right?" said one of the detectives.

"Kind of," I said. "Very old. A collector would pay top dollar."

"Well, you know who's got it, then. Teflon Tim."

"You think?"

"Sure. He's not dumb. Talks like a lawyer. And for a pimp, he's not an absolute fucking prick, you know? I bet he took the book in return for paying her rent for six months or something."

"Yeah," said the other. "Freeing up the cash for her to pay her buddy to shoot her ass full of caulk."

"That makes a disgusting kind of sense," I said. "So where do I find Teflon Tim?"

Chapter 38

There's a fucked-up shitpipe in the men's room," said the bouncer as we slid through the knifemarked door into the bar. The place stank of weed and puke and shit. Two ceiling lights out of every three had been smashed out, jagged glass glinting in the fixtures.

"We're looking for Muppet," I said, as the two cops had suggested.

The bouncer looked us over, distaste in his big stitched-up face. "Business or pleasure?"

"Strictly business."

"Good. Turn around." The bouncer patted me down professionally.

"Inside jacket pocket," he growled. I held the right side of my jacket open for him.

"It's a handheld computer," I said. "Lift it out and

check it." He slid it out carefully, spun it in his hands until he found the release button, and opened it up.

"Huh. What does it do?"

"Email. Games."

"Okay." He handed it back to me and then checked Trix; no attempt to cop a feel. The guy had been trained properly, somewhere official. I wouldn't push my luck with him.

Satisfied, he asked if we knew what Muppet looked like.

"No," I said. "You already worked out we're not local. We talk to him and we leave. That's the whole deal."

"Good. Far end of the bar, red hair, eyes like you never saw on a human being before. Buy a drink, no acting out, and I don't got a problem with you being here."

I thanked him and we headed to the bar. The guy the cops called Muppet was there, all right. Hair like red yarn, red eyebrows that you'd need a whip and a chair to put in their place, eyes that stood out of his face like someone had slipped boiled eggs into his sockets. Wearing a wifebeater so old and thin that you could see his ribs through it, so scrawny you could practically see his heart behind his ribs. Jogging pants covered in tiny little burn holes and stinking of dope, and shiny new running shoes.

We ordered drinks and watched him for a little bit. I

wanted to get his measure. Every few minutes his pocket played the riff from "Axel F," and he fished a cell phone out from it. It always came out with scraps of tissue stuck to it by velcro snot. He'd rattle off numbers in a reedy voice and then shove it back. Take a few deep pulls of beer. Repeat.

The fifth time the phone went back, I approached him. Muppet immediately fixed me with awesomely bloodshot eyes.

"You're Muppet?" I said.

"Muppet," he agreed.

"Cop," he said.

"Private detective. There's no trouble here. I'm look-ing to talk with Tim about buying something he recently came into possession of. Straight business deal, no cops, no angles."

"Tell Muppet. Muppet tell him."

"I get to talk directly to him tonight, you get a finder's fee. My client authorized five grand."

His red eyes wheeled about in his head. "Fifteen."

"Ten." Which was the number I was going to start with, before I got a look at him.

"Now."

"When I've got what I want. I can't get the cash out of the client otherwise."

"Now."

"Can't do it."

"Now."

"Forget it," I said, and turned away, collecting Trix's hand in mine.

"Where you going?" Muppet whined.

"Cops," I said. "I was keeping them out of it, dealing on the level. But if you're going to be a prick about it, I'm going to talk to a couple of friends on the force. They'll pick him up on a bogus charge and put him in a cell long enough for me to talk to him. My buddies will split eight grand, which leaves two for me as a little bonus. And when Tim asks exactly who fucked up to the extent that he's spending a night in a cell with some AIDS-infested assrapist, I'll tell him it was you. I'm dealing straight with you, but I'm not going to be fucked with."

Muppet folded in on himself, scowling. "Muppet sad."

"Have a nice night," I said, and started walking.

"Okay," he piped, pulling his phone.

"You're funny when you try to be a hardass," Trix whispered. I trod on her foot.

Chapter 39

Christ, I want a gun," I heard myself say.

The address Muppet gave us, after an interminable time on the phone where he explained the situation to Tim Cardinal in the style of fucking Sesame Street, appeared to be an abandoned water utility plant. Huge filthy pumps stood dead, there wasn't a light on in the place, and it all felt like trouble.

"You think he's maybe a touch paranoid?" Trix smiled.

We found the open door to the main building, as described by Muppet. There was a heavy flashlight laid on the floor waiting for us. I switched it on and lit up a place that looked like it'd been abandoned with two minutes' notice. Mugs of coffee still on tables, over-flowing with vivid green mold. In the messroom, fungus crawled off plates left midmeal, skewed cutlery half-buried in the moss. Here and there, coats still hung on hooks.

We had our instructions. We went down. Rusted metal staircases rung dissonantly. The wet stone floors deadened all the sound. Even our footsteps rang wrong.

Two levels down, we found the door we were looking for, an *X* roughly scratched into its steel. There was an odd light beyond. I went through first, shifting my grip down to the base of the flashlight so I could use it as a blackjack if necessary.

The door was an access point to a wide, wet, stinking tunnel. My attention was drawn to the floor. The light came from a couple of dozen shake-and-break green glowsticks tossed on the ground.

And I was looking at those instead of everything else. Trix yelped.

I turned. There was a gun muzzle pushed into her eye.

A tall, thin man with bad skin and eyes like a doll's was behind her, one arm around her throat, the other pressing a gun into her eye.

"The thing about cheap bullets," he said, "is that they'll shatter on the inside of her skull. I can shoot her through the brain and the bullet will not emerge out of the other side. My name's Tim Cardinal. I understand you wanted to see me."

Dead eyes. They didn't reflect any light. Black and motionless. His smile was polite and without life.

"This was business," I said.

His polite smile widened by a precise amount, as if he'd learned how to feign emotions in the mirror. "This is how I do business. I have no desire to kill her. But then, I have no desire to use toilets or eat food. They are simply things I have to do in order to live. So is this. You wanted to see me?"

"Trix, just relax," I said. "We're doing business here. He's not going to have any reason to harm you."

"You think he needs a reason?" she said.

Tim Cardinal laughed. It made me jump: it sounded like a gunshot in a small room. "Oh, I like you. Now. I won't ask again. You wanted to see me?"

I put the flashlight beam square on his face. I wanted him to focus on me, not Trix.

"Alexis Perez received a book as payment from a client," I said, in as loud and steady a voice as I could manage with Trix looking down a gun barrel. "I believe you took the book for yourself. It's a rare antique. My client has hired and empowered me to purchase it from you for a significant fee. Under-the-table purchase, bank transfer, no records."

"How do you do a bank transfer with no records?" Cardinal sneered.

"My client is very important. It's not an issue. I'm here to give you a lot of money for a book that's no good to you. There's no need for any of this."

"If the book is so very important to your very important client, how do I know it's no good to me?"

"Are you intending to go into politics any time soon?"

He laughed again, a genuine snort of amusement. The tunnel still made it a flat and horrible noise. "No."

"Then it's no good to you."

He considered. "This would be the old leatherbound thing that she got from the Texan?"

"Right."

"And she told you I had it?"

"She's dead. She died a few hours ago. Death by misadventure. Home-brew plastic surgery."

"Oh," he said. For a moment there, he almost looked concerned. And then, "So how do you know I have it? Who told you?"

"I'm a detective. I worked it out. Let go of her now."

"No."

"Why not?"

"Because you want me to. You're not armed, are you?"

"No." Damnit.

He threw the smile away, but there was light in his eyes for the first time. He was amused. He had all the power in the situation, and he knew it, and that was the only thing in the world that could make him register a pulse.

"I don't have the book," he said.

"Then we'll be on our way. No hard feelings, no comeback. You won't see us again."

"But you have money, don't you?"

"Not with me. Who has the book?"

"Ah. I have *two* things you want, then. What price do you set on that name and her life?"

"Screw the name. Let her go."

Cardinal grinned. "I am finding this very interesting. I think I'm going to kill you both. Her first. Let you watch. Would that be nice?"

"I have access to four hundred thousand dollars," I said.

"Where is it?"

"In a bank account. It's yours if you let her go."

Trix's jaw dropped.

"And how do I get this money? Do we go into a bank together? I don't think so."

Shit. I thought furiously, trying to find a way to make this work.

"Mike," Trix said in a small voice. "The handheld."

"There's a handheld computer in my inside jacket pocket," I said. "It connects to the Internet. I can get to my account through it. I'm going to take it out, very slowly, okay?"

I opened my jacket wide and carefully extracted the device with two fingers. He watched me like a hawk the whole time. I snapped it open and began pressing buttons. The net connection coughed a bit—I was a little surprised it even worked, being two floors underground—but it got to the online banking thing. I was all fingers and thumbs, and I barely understood the fucking thing to begin with. I held it out.

"Trix is better with this thing than I am."

He thought about this. I was visibly trembling. He liked it. Cardinal withdrew the gun from her eye and carefully placed it at the back of her head, at arm's length. "Do it," he said to her.

Trix took the handheld and began keying it, quickly and precisely. She cocked her head toward Cardinal. "What's your account number?"

Amused, he gave her the number and codes, and she keyed them in with superb focus. Handed the device over her shoulder to him. "Check it."

He took the device, and spent a few moments studying it. The light from the glowsticks was fading now, and his drawn features were lit coldly by the screen.

"Well, now," he eventually said. "It appears that your bank account is empty and mine is full."

"It's nonreversible," Trix said. "It's marked as such at the bottom of the page there. You've got the money and we can't take it away from you."

Cardinal passed the handheld back over Trix's shoulder.

"It has been a pleasure doing business with you both." He fished in his coat pocket for something. The glow was almost dead, and I played my flashlight over him as he rummaged. He produced a matchbook.

"Before you arrived, I wrote the name and address of the entity I sold the book to on this. I prefer to be fully prepared for all eventualities, no matter how outlandish. So should you."

The last of the glowsticks died. He tossed the matchbook on the ground. I put the flashlight on it. When I brought the beam back up to find Cardinal, he was gone. His footsteps stolen by the wet stone.

Chapter 40

Back in the car, Trix couldn't stop shaking. She tried a weak smile on me. "Suddenly, this isn't so much fun."

"I told you I hate Las Vegas," I said, cranking the ignition.

"Hold on a second," she said. "You just gave someone four hundred thousand dollars to save my life."

Because I'm an asshole, I said, "Well, it wasn't *my* four hundred grand."

"Yes, it was. If we don't get the book, that payment is all you're ever going to see from this job. And you just blew it all. For me."

"Let's be honest. I only would've drunk it. And I put you in that situation in the first place."

She laughed, and it was more like a rattle. "I think it was the first time you didn't ask me to stay in the car."

"See? My fault." I threw the gearshift and pulled away. "And now I have to figure how to get us to L.A. with no money."

"There was more than four hundred in the account. I shunted the change into my own account before I sent the four hundred to his."

I thought about this. "Well, that was probably what I owed you, anyway."

"So? I'm your partner. We'll use it to get the job done."

"That's your money, Trix."

"It's not my money, just like it wasn't yours. Right?"

"Shouldn't you be in shock or something?" I said.

That brought her all the way back. She punched me in the arm, and then slumped back in her seat. "Jesus, what a night. I'm never coming back here again. You said something about L.A.?"

I blew out stale air. "Yeah. That prick sold the book to a law firm in Los Angeles, would you believe."

"You're kidding me."

"Nope."

"I know a lawyer in L.A. In fact, I bet we could stay with him. Which is just as well, as I highly doubt we can afford swanky hotels now."

"What can we afford?"

She grinned. "You ever skipped out of a hotel without paying before?"

Chapter 41

And then, with the board in the bed ripped out and a pair of panties dangling off Jesus' face, she kissed me, warm and tender and long like she'd never kissed me before, and whispered, "You saved my life. You gave up on the book and the job and the money to save my life. I could fall in love with you."

I've said I love you when I've meant it, and I've said I love you when it was the right thing to say, and I've said I love you when saying anything else would have hurt someone without reason. And I couldn't say a word, there in the dark.

Chapter 42

We snuck out of the back of the hotel and caught a bus to the airport, where Trix bought a couple of coach tickets to LAX. She took the cell phone to call her friend, apparently getting nothing but the answering machine. She'd turned away from me and muttered what seemed like an absurdly detailed message into the phone.

After that, it was down to an hour of waiting, leaning on each other in the hard plastic departure-lounge chairs, tired and stressed and silent. I put one eye on a nearby TV, which was showing choppy, pixelated footage from the war in the Middle East. Blood on the road. Bumpy handheld camerawork. An American soldier who was maybe twenty, crying, screaming at what I guess was his commanding officer. The sound was turned down, so all you got was this kid dressed as a soldier with blood all over his uniform shrieking silently.

A fat guy lumbered past with one of those little suitcases on wheels. The case didn't seem to be big enough to contain one pair of the underpants that guy must've needed. On the case was slapped a glossy plastic sticker demanding that I SUPPORT OUR TROOPS. Looking at the shocky commander not knowing what to say to the screaming soldier, I came to the decision that I'd start that just as soon as I saw *our troops* supporting our troops. It didn't do much for my mood.

I elbowed a small child in the face so that Trix could get a window seat, and she fell asleep while I was still apologizing to its obese, dirt-streaked mother. When the flight attendant came to intercede, I told her the mother was yelling at me in Iraqi, and she and her poison spawn were frogmarched off the plane.

I sat next to Trix, and a musty-smelling middle-aged man with a hawk's profile arranged himself in the aisle seat next to me. His houndstooth suit had been second-hand when God was a boy, and what I first took for badly maintained spats turned out, on closer inspection, to be cut-down gray gym socks arranged over battered black Chelsea boots.

After takeoff, Trix went off to sleep, a trick I was learning to resent if not despise her for.

The man next to me looked down his nose at me and took a long, pipe-clearing sniff. "You look weary. A traveling man?"

"You could say that. New York, Columbus, San Antonio, Vegas. On to L.A."

He wriggled with pleasure at the prospect. "What a crooked little vein you travel. All the way to the heart of America. The red, steaming valves of Los Angeles. A fine place for a detective to be headed."

I got that little see-saw feeling in my stomach when something I can't put my finger on is wrong. Like knowing something's waiting around the corner for me with big teeth and a hard-on. "How did you know I'm a detective?"

"You have the smell on you. The smell of Crime. I, too, am in the life. A consulting detective. Falconer's the name. Perhaps you've heard of me?"

"Um . . . no."

"But I was recently featured in *The Investigator's Companion.*"

"I don't know what that is."

"The *Companion*? The monthly journal for detectives?"

"Never heard of it."

"Aaah. That explains it. I am *Falconer*, boy! I am the

world's greatest consulting detective. I, sir, am the man who solved a crime by placing the deceased victim's penis in my mouth."

"You sucked the corpse off."

"Don't be so disgusting," Falconer said. "No wonder you don't read the *Companion.* You are plainly some kind of hired pervert. I simply needed to learn of the woman who had sex with him before he died. My early years as a male prostitute have gifted me with exceedingly sharp senses and a preternaturally strong tongue. By tasting the cadaver's todger, I could tell not only that the woman used an extremely strong spermicide—which robbed me of the use of my lips for some moments—but also that the woman's vagina had a uniquely horrible flavor. This led directly to a female user and dealer of amphetamine sulphate—which quite ruins the taste of a woman's secretions—posing as a vagrant prostitute to entrap and murder the man."

I accidentally on purpose kicked Trix in the ankle. She didn't wake up. I hated her.

"Not the strangest crime I ever prosecuted, of course," Falconer said, picking his nose. "Imagine the scene: A slender, flat-chested girl with a small bottom covered entirely in blood, and a very old man on the floor with no penis at all. And only I, the great consulting detective, possessed of supernatural skills honed by years as a professional lover of all mammals, could possibly solve this case. Anus dentata, would you believe."

"A . . . what?"

"Anus dentata. Rare, but all too real. The old gentleman on the floor with no undercarriage preferred to take his pleasure through the tradesman's entrance. However, the poor girl's anal teeth would snap shut involuntarily upon local muscular stimulation. Severing and quite possibly devouring the bishop's erection."

"The bishop."

"Oh, good God, yes. The girl, possessed of a boyish figure, had been wearing a school uniform that featured a trouser rather than a skirt. The unfortunate and unpenised man of God was attempting to wean himself off choirboys. It would be sad if, frankly, it were not so very funny. What sort of cases do you pursue?"

"Divorces. Ostrich abuse. Tantric bestiality."

"Oh! A kindred spirit! A brother in the damp corridors of sexual invention and the romance of Crime! Did you hear about the Red Shoes Killer?"

"No."

"Four crack whores found sticking out of a washing machine. Their feet had been lightly grated, and then they'd been forced to dance on a floorspace thinly dusted with finest cocaine. The killer, you see, was a lecturer in English Literature, both hedonistic and hebephrenic. Someone attempting, misguidedly, to empower childlike behavior through vice. *The Red Shoes*! You remember it? "'Dance you shall,' said he, 'dance in your red shoes till you are pale and cold, till your skin shrivels up and you are a skeleton!'" A fairy tale. Consider the scene again: blood leaking from tortured soles stung with cocaine, forcing motion? Blood-slicked feet, my brother detective—red shoes."

"Look, I have had a really shitty night. I've gone along with this as long as I could, because it's basically my punishment from God or something and I've learned to live with and accept it. But you are just blatantly making shit up now, and I'd like you to stop."

Falconer squared his shoulders and gave me his contemptuous profile. "If you were a reader of the *Companion*—which is to say, if you were a *proper* detective, sir—you would know that Falconer invents nothing. The cases I pursue are simply too unusual and horrible to make it into the electronic media. But they are not hidden, sir, no. They are *published*. They are the stuff of mainstream consideration within our sainted trade. And they are *not invented*."

He bullshitted on the subject for a while longer. Something still felt wrong. It wasn't the usual weirdness index of my life. Something else. A bomb not dropped.

". . . the police scientists confirmed that the placenta filling the gullet of the dead girl strapped to the bed once shared a womb with the live boy who nursed his testicular wounds. It had been cleverly preserved by a master criminal for precisely this purpose—choking the boy's girlfriend to death. Said master criminal being the boy's mother, of course."

"Mr. Falconer?"

"One moment, young man. As I said, both parties bore the mark of a hypodermic syringe. My supposition was that the boy's mother entered the house while he was engaged in coitus with the young lady. She assaulted them both with a hypodermic syringe charged with a substance that made them both more . . . pliant. She was restrained, and the placenta shoved into her mouth. She choked to death while the mother tied him into a hard wooden chair and rrrrutted with him until blood vessels under his scrotum burst against repeated violent contact with its edge. Crime and sex are inextricably linked, I have found."

"I was wondering—"

"I'm sure you were. You're a bright young man. She did indeed force her son to ejaculate into a plastic drip-feed bag such as is found in medical establishments, later to introduce his vigorous sperm into her blood-stream for the purpose of youth preservation. I suspect she bred him specifically for sexual entertainment and, in her twisted mind, the production of age-retarding chemicals. The girl was killed as instruction and punishment: you belong only to Mummy. The most fascinating detail, I believe, were the ligatures on his thighs—left, quite literally, by his mother's apron strings. I considered meeting the woman, you know. A schoolboy's uniform and some kind of cricket box to protect my precious scrotal treasures, and I would have been in like Flynn."

"Why are you going to Los Angeles, Mr. Falconer?"

He broke into a beatific grin. "The game is afoot, my young colleague. I have learned of a sexual demimonde in Los Angeles."

"No kidding."

"Oh yes. But not the usual thing, no. These aren't pissdrinkers or vomit-fellatio specialists, no no. I am talking of parties wherein persons possessed of certain diseases have young things from foreign climes shipped in for their filthy pleasures, and then take bets on which of them will die of the transmitted infections."

"That's horrible."

"And one of these persons holds in false ownership a certain statuette, avian in appearance, hailing from

Malta. My services have been engaged to retrieve the bird and—"

I fished my lighter out of my pocket and passed it to him. "Hold this for a second, would you?"

"Of course."

He took the lighter. I punched him repeatedly in the face, and then told the flight attendants and surrounding passengers that I'd seen Falconer trying to set light to something in his shoes.

By the time we began to orbit LAX, Falconer's face looked like bad steak. Everyone had had a go, even the old lady from five rows back, who tore up a plastic drinks tumbler and slashed him like she was a street fighter. I opened up a vomit bag and pulled it over his head. Trix slept through the whole thing.

Chapter 43

Leaning over Trix, I looked out at Los Angeles. An orange bowl inverted over the city. From a distance, you wonder how anyone can live there.

Stop-start shuffling our way through LAX security into Arrivals, she spotted something and pointed to me. An Asian girl in a business suit behind the cattle-fencing human funnel that pours people out into the hall, holding a clipboard with TRIX +1 scrawled in marker on the top sheet.

Trix grabbed my hand and tugged me through the crowds to the girl. "I'm Trix Holmes, and this is my plus-one. Brom sent you?"

The girl showed us a row of bleached teeth. I wouldn't call it a smile. "Well, hi. I'm Blair? Brom's assistant? I'm to drive you out to the house? Follow me?"

Bone-chilling air-conditioning gave way to a sweat-and grime-laden wall of hot air as we got out onto the street. I actually took a step back from the force of it. Blair struck out across the street like a native guide, giving the finger to cabs and limos as she strode toward the short-stay parking lot. A neutral silver SUV bleeped hello to her keychain, and she left us to throw our bags into the trunk and clamber in.

"I'm going to have to leave you at the house? I'm running late for my vaginal tightening appointment?"

Trix frowned. "Honey, you're twenty-one if you're a day. There's no way in hell your vagina needs anything of the sort. Besides, everyone's a different size. It's just nature."

Blair turned around in her chair and looked Trix up and down as if considering a circus freak. "Yeah, well. You're from *New York.*"

Trix looked at me like it was my fault and leaned back in the chair. It was a long drive. On and off freeways, wending up and down ramp roads. My attention would drift, and then I'd look back out the window and have no idea where we were. Blair wasn't in the mood for a guided tour, and just shrugged her shoulders at every question. Her mind was obviously on the minutes ticking away toward her prized vaginal tuck.

An hour of this, and we pulled up in front of a blindingly white house perched on the edge of what looked like a cliff face, looking down on the valley of Los Angeles. I got out of the car first, eager to relieve my aching ass. The light was beautiful. I never realized, until I was there, exactly why the movie business settled out there. It wasn't just getting out of New York and living an economic version of the Wild West. Up there, over the smog line, the light had a sharp clarity that would have made a painter cry. Somehow, though, I figured every artist in L.A. was probably down there under the orange, cutting up sheep and making funny boxes and calling that art instead.

I tried explaining the thought to Trix, but she told me about the acquaintance of hers down there who performed his art by breaking into abandoned hospitals and reenacted horrifying nineteenth-century medical procedures with morbidly obese mental patients and strippers covered in blood.

Blair let us into the house. The hallway looked like a four-star hotel lobby. Blair explained that Brom was tied up for much of the day, but wanted us to treat the house as ours until he got home. She gave us the once-over one more time, as if judging how much of Brom's stuff we could steal, and then took off at a brusque speed, eager for stitches in her nether regions.

Once the door was shut, I made a show of looking around. "Your friend does okay for himself, huh?"

"Brom's very successful. Takes on big corporate cases to fund pro bono civil-liberties cases. He used to be in New York, fighting Giuliani. Moved out here after 9/11."

"Good friend of yours?"

"We dated a little bit, I guess. He's a very good friend, yeah."

"Uh-huh."

"Mike, we had this conversation. Are you going to be weird about this?"

"No, no. Just tired. It's been a bad couple of days, you know?"

"You're telling me."

"You're coping pretty well."

She grinned and kissed me fast and hard. "Why shouldn't I? You saved me."

"Just remember that when your lawyer ex wants to do pro bono in your pants."

"Beats paying rent. *I'm joking.* Quit looking like you just shit yourself."

"I'm going to go exploring for food. If I'm not back in a couple of days, call the police. I may have gotten lost in this guy's closet or something."

Chapter 44

Are edamame food?"

"Sure," Trix called from the living room, about two miles away from me in the kitchen. "It's a bean. You steam them and have them with rock salt."

I replaced the bag of green things that had been left artfully on the counter and went back to grubbing around the cupboards in the vast brushed-steel kitchen. Piles of unopened packets and boxes of alien things that could possibly be food, and stacks of books about the Atkins and GI diets. I wasn't totally convinced that Trix's friend ever actually cooked in here. Nothing seemed to have been used, and things were arranged for aesthetic pleasure more than utility. This was a guy that ate out a lot.

Since Trix wasn't in sight, I went through the drawers.

A sheaf of bills in the first drawer, each one bearing a Post-it note saying that an assistant had paid it. The sheaf sat a little high, for the depth of the drawer. I pulled the sheaf out. The drawer had a false bottom, a DIY job held in by two clips. I popped the left-hand clip and lifted the thin wooden sheet up. There was a handgun, a new leather shoulder holster, and a slim box of ammunition underneath. The gun's license documentation was laid underneath it.

I have some knowledge of guns from the Chicago days. I don't particularly like them. That said, I've never met a lot of people in law enforcement or the investigative business who did. Cops tend to view them as tools. Detectives tend to see them either as insurance or, on many occasions, an excuse to be shot at. The guys who like guns are usually the ones found on slabs with ballistics geeks tweezering lumps of pulped metal out of their chests.

I smiled at this gun. It was a Ruger Super Blackhawk, .44 Magnum. I met the famous detective Jay Armes at an investigators' conference once. He had hooks for hands—his original hands had been blown off by a box of railroad torpedoes when he was a kid, and legend had it that he'd gotten a pistol built into one of the hooks—frightening hair, and a jacket that hurt my eyes. He'd been shot at by a .44, and he said that the joke about the Super Blackhawk, back in the fifties when it was first launched, was that it was a great gun for holding up trains. You just fired the gun at the train and it stopped. It's a huge, heavy piece of blued metal, a six-shot revolver—not an I-need-a-gun-to-protect-my-property kind of gun. The long barrel, the great big bullets, and the sheer weight of the thing damping off the recoil makes the Super Blackhawk an extraordinarily accurate, one-shot-stopper of a gun. Even if that huge damn bullet somehow doesn't kill you, the rocket force of the impact kicks you clean off your feet. These days, it's mostly used as a hunter's handgun. Though God knows what you'd hunt with it. Anything smaller than a rhino would probably splatter like God himself reached down from the clouds and punched it in the head.

This was a guy who wanted a nice big retro-style gun. A six-shooter, no less. With a shoulder holster, even, that still reeked of new leather and creaked when I pressed on it. I bet he put it on and posed with it in the mirror every now and then. Someone should have told him that Travis Bickle was from New York and Dirty Harry was from San Francisco and neither of them would have been caught dead in Los Angeles.

I replaced the sheet carefully.

The fridge was the size of a car. I found some fruit in

the bottom bin, and piled bananas, clementines, apples, and passion fruit on a plate, grabbing a knife and a couple of spoons before walking it through to Trix.

Trix was in front of the widescreen TV, watching a local news report about a blind man who'd been arrested for raping his guide dog.

I laid the fruit next to her. "Sometimes I almost understand why that old bastard wants to use the book on America," I smiled.

Trix picked up a clementine and started skinning it without looking away from the screen. "I don't even get how he's going to do it. Read it out on TV?"

"Apparently he can't do that. You have to be in the actual presence of the book, to get the subsonic effect or something. They'll take it from town to town, like the Freedom Train in the seventies. Big public gatherings. Putting the reset button to all you weirdos one crowd at a time."

Trix flipped a segment of clementine into her mouth. "Will that work?"

"He seems to think so. I mean, unless this is all one big costly joke at my expense."

"You have to admit that's possible."

"Yeah. No. I don't think so. Not this time. He really believes it. And, you know, he might be crazy, but he's not stupid."

Trix chewed and considered. "I don't think you should give him the book."

"Why not?"

"Okay. Assume this isn't totally nuts and this book can somehow affect people's brains. Is it right that the government should be able to reset people's personalities to some two-hundred-year-old notion of 'morality'?"

I sliced off some apple. "Because people should be free to rape their own guide dogs any time they like?"

"Aside from the fact that there are many, many working bestiality relationships in America today—"

"You're kidding me."

"There was a TV documentary about it last year."

"That's not exactly anyone's idea of a mainstream society, Trix."

"Says who? It's on national TV and it's not mainstream? This *is* the mainstream. This is how life is."

"You're going to sit there and defend dogfucking as a lifestyle choice?"

"Why do I have to defend it? Why not just accept that such relationships exist and then ensure that abuse isn't taking place?"

"Fucking a dog isn't abusing a dog?"

"Why not find out first, before condemning it? Adult animals crossbreed all the time. When I was a kid, my rabbit and my guinea pig were shafting each other senseless every season. It's not like we're talking about pre-sexual beings."

"Trix, you are seriously defending people who fuck animals here."

"I'm saying there's more going on in the modern psyche than can be defined by some Puritan notion of the way life should be. Hell, in the last couple of weeks I've done things to you that are still illegal in some states. The pace of change in the way we live isn't limited to the number of consumer products available, Mike. Hell, look at the way porn's changed."

"I know. I saw a TV show with the guy who invented anal sex."

"I kind of doubt that. But, you know, some women can't get off vaginally. Some women can't get off without a bit of the rough stuff. Porn doesn't invent that. It reflects what's going on in the world. And some bad easy-listening music and ten minutes of vanilla missionary doesn't do it for everybody. Using that book in the middle of any major city would be consigning thousands of people to hell every time."

I stabbed my last slice of apple. "So you're saying me finding the book would make the transcontinental pervert community very unhappy, and that they would conceivably be forced to unlearn all their special pervert tricks."

"Mike, you're talking about lobotomizing people. Think about it: what would that book do to me?"

"You wouldn't want to make me ejaculate into the Baby Jesus' head anymore."

"Two hundred years ago, the female orgasm was mostly theoretical. Hell, a hundred years ago, the male psyche didn't have a problem with selling women. We barely got educated. Career aspirations, forget it. The *1950s* looked like fucking Babylon compared to 1776. Everything that makes me *me*, Mike, would be wiped away. Gimme the knife."

"With that look in your eye? I don't think I want you to have the knife."

"What, you're afraid I'm going to put it up your ass and call it romance? Gimme the fucking knife."

I watched as she pushed the apples and oranges onto a nearby coffee table, unzipped the bananas onto the plate, sliced them, cut the passion fruit, and squeezed the pulp all over them. She started eating the mess with one of the spoons, watching the TV.

There were no ashtrays visible in the place, so I decided to press some clementine peel into service and lit up. "You don't think maybe they just want to make America a less freakier place?"

Trix eyed me, crunching a passion fruit seed. "Three thousand years ago stable homosexual relationships were mainstream in many societies all over the world. Don't you think the current administration would consider that kind of freaky?"

"Three thousand years ago people painted themselves blue and hunted their own food with sticks. Don't treat me like I'm an idiot, Trix."

"What's your point?"

"My point is that maybe, just maybe, America would get along fine without people who fuck dogs."

"So you're equating stable homosexual relationships with dogfucking."

"Actually, no. *You* are. So why don't you put down your studenty bullshit for one minute and talk to me like an adult?"

"Oh, fuck you, Mike. Maybe it's a bigger subject than two people can deal with over breakfast, okay?"

"Well, guess what. It *is* down to two people. Sometimes that's the way it breaks. And it can be down to one person if you like."

"What's that supposed to mean?"

"You can go home any time you like." Goddamn moron that I was.

"So you can hand over this thing with a clear conscience?"

"Oh, so you're Jiminy fucking Cricket now. No. So I can just get the job done with the minimum amount of distraction and then go home myself. You may not have noticed, but *I am not having fun here*, Trix. This job started out weird and it's gotten scary. I want it to be over now. Either I don't find the book, in which case I'm going to assume this is the end of the line, or I find the book, in which case I hand it the hell over, get paid, go home, and forget the whole thing ever happened."

She looked at me with narrowed eyes. "You want to forget it all happened."

"Yeah," I said, like a goddamn moron, "yeah, I do."

"Uh-huh. You know, I was wondering how this'd start to go wrong. I didn't really think it'd begin with me daring to have an opinion."

"What?"

"You want to forget it all happened? That starts with me, Mike. Look at you. Did you even realize you stood up? Your chin sticking out like a sulky child? Your fists all balled up?"

"I didn't mean—"

"Sure you did. And, you know, if you really think handing over anything that could even possibly affect people's minds to the bastard in the White House is a good idea—or if you care so little about people that you really don't give a shit whether it's a good idea or not—then maybe it's just as well I'm getting a good look at you now. Give me the handheld."

"What for?"

"I want to take some pictures and upload them to my photo-hosting site."

Why the hell not. I took it out of my jacket and dropped it on the carpet by her.

"Do what you like, Trix. If you really, honestly think I was talking about us, when the whole conversation had been about the job . . . then fuck it. I'll get my stuff and find a hotel. And you can do what you like. This is a stupid argument. You're talking yourself around in circles and I just want to get done with this *job* that has scared the shit out of me and go back to some semblance of a life. With you, if you can get past the fact that it's you I care about and not the endless parade of assholes, freaks, and crapsacks I meet every day. Without you, if you really believe my lack of love for the animal-humping community is a good enough reason to throw us away. I'm going out for a walk. You do what you like."

Chapter 45

I walked for an hour before I realized I no longer remembered what I was so pissed about. By which point I was totally lost and had no idea how to get back to the house.

So I lit up a cigarette (and I knew I was smoking too much), slowed down, and just strolled for a while, to see where the broad sunlit streets led me. Every now and then I stopped at a corner and looked around for a cab, reminding myself each time that I wasn't in New York and that this wasn't a civilized city.

Occasionally, a private car would go by, and I'd see faces pressed to the windows, staring at me like I was an alien. It eventually hit me that I was the only pedestrian I'd seen the whole time I was pounding the sidewalk, and that I stood out like a cheerleader in Riker's.

I just walked. After a while, houses gave way to low,

broad industrial units. I stopped on a corner to light another cigarette, just because I really was in that kind of a mood. It took me a moment to register someone yelling at me. I was about to yell back that smoking was still allowed outdoors when I realized the guy doing the shouting, standing at the entrance to the nearest industrial building, was waving an unlit cigarette. He was stocky, midthirties, glasses, and a *Star Wars* T-shirt that looked like it'd been printed when the first one came out. He was scratching at his short brown hair like a little monkey that'd been kept in a cage too long. I wandered over.

"Please tell me you've got a light," he said in a strangled voice. "My lighter died and I swear no one in the entire building smokes anymore."

I flicked my lighter and cupped the flame for him. He sucked at his smoke like a dehydrated kid putting a straw to a lake. None of the smoke came back out of him, as if his body had just absorbed the entire load. "Thanks, man. I was dying. People always said these things would kill me."

"No problem."

He stuck out a stubby-fingered hand. "Zack. Zack Pickles."

"Mike McGill." I nodded at the building. "This your business?"

"Yep. Welcome to the Farm." He had a goofy, child-like grin that made me kind of like him right off the bat.

"What kind of business?"

"Internet business. You?"

"I'm a private investigator." I laughed as he instantly turned paler than ghost shit. "Relax. I'm not from around here, I'm already on a case, and I never heard of you. I'm staying with a friend of a friend . . . hell, somewhere back over there, I'm a little bit kind of totally fucking lost at this point. And it's a lost property case. So, you know, go me. You can restart your heart now."

"That obvious?"

"'Fraid so. Whatever your business is, I give you my word I couldn't care less."

He blew out a breath, sagging in his skin. "Jesus. This is why I don't leave the server room. You're from out of town?"

"Manhattan." I struggled my wallet out and gave him one of my few remaining business cards. The ones that survived going around the washing machine six weeks earlier. "The trail led me here, though I don't hold out a hell of a lot of hope. And, well, I think I just fucked things up with a girl, and I'm walking, and . . ."

"And here you are. Girls are nothing but trouble anyway. They are not like us."

"This one especially. Trust me."

He grinned. "You look like a man who could use a drink. And I never met a real live PI before. You want a beer?"

"That is the first sane thing I've heard all day."

"C'mon. I'll give you the ten-cent tour."

We went into the building's lobby, where I was blasted half to death by L.A.-style arctic air-conditioning. A sour-looking girl gave me a handwritten visitor's badge on a lanyard stolen from an adult movie expo in 2001 at Zack's request.

"So what do you farm here, Zack?"

"Money. Information. Also cum."

Pushing through the big double doors at the end of the lobby, we entered a massive space filled with three-walled cubicles. I leaned around the missing wall of the first one. The cubicle had been made to look like a teenager's bed-room. On the single bed was a young woman in schoolgirl gear and a headset preparing to do something disgusting and probably quite painful with a pink rubber dildo the size of my entire arm. There was a laptop on the bed next to her. Set in the doorway was a camera on a tripod, thick cables running out of it and chasing into the floor.

I looked at Zack. "The hell?"

He pointed ahead, smiling proudly. Every cubicle I looked in had a similar arrangement. Some of them replaced girls with boys. A few had boys dressed as girls. One had a woman in her late sixties. The only cubicle with two people in it featured a pair of Japanese girls doing something just frighteningly hideous with a bucket of baby eels. Every last one of them was performing sex acts in front of a dedicated camera.

We went through the next set of heavy double doors, into a corridor.

"What did I just see, Zack?"

"One part of my business. Cool, no?"

"I don't know. I don't know what I just saw."

"Okay. You go to one of my Web sites. The Web site connects to the laptops in the cubes. The girl with the laptop performs to the camera. The camera connects to the Net. The video from the cam shoots down the Net to the Web site. You see the girl in the cube. The whole thing's on a ten-second delay. The signal basically wraps around the world before it comes to your computer. Legal reasons, I'm not going into it. You pay for the video by credit card, I sanitize the sale in Russia, we're all good."

"But . . . Why so many? Jesus Christ, man, why the *eels*?"

Zack giggled. "Because everyone has a different kink, man. The more Web sites with unique content I provide, the more customers I get. Not everyone gets off on a softcore murder mystery on Skinemax, you know? And once the infrastructure was down, adding new sites was almost costless."

"Kinda fringe-y, though, surely? I mean, girls with eels in their . . . Is there a lot of call for that?"

"Think of it as exploded television. Every station has at least one show you want to see, right? Well, on my network, your favorite show is on all the time. Everyone's favorite show is on all the time, whenever you want to watch it. Add up all the viewers on my network, and I have a bigger audience than HBO. This ain't fringe anymore, friend. If you define the mainstream as that which most people want to watch, then I'm as mainstream as it gets."

"Exploded television."

"Exactly. Exploded television. I am the *ultra* cable company. This is the way of the future. Anything you want, on a computer screen, whenever you want it, through a subscription or a micropayment of a few bucks through your credit card. That eel thing? For a buck a time you can download the day's highlights to your iPod and watch it while you're in the can. *Huge* in Japan. And it pays for all kinds of interesting stuff."

"Whoa. Hold up." I wanted a minute to catch up with this. "You've got like fifty people in wired-up video Internet sex boxes out there . . . and that's not the whole thing?"

"It's not even the whole of the cubicle farm. We've got another hundred people upstairs."

"Yeah, I get that you have a porn army in here. But

you're leading me to believe that this isn't all about you getting richer than God. Because if you're not bullshitting me then you have got to be richer than God."

Zack opened the nearest door and gestured for me to go in. "Oh, hell, yeah. I could buy Paris Hilton and sell her body to medical science while she was still alive if I wanted to. And, believe me, there are times I've considered it. In here."

The door led only to a small gray cell with another door, much heavier, on the opposite wall. This one had a keypad lock. Zack made a sheepish face as he shielded the keypad with his body to input the number code that popped the door. And pop it did, with a hiss: hermetically sealed.

It opened on what I can only describe as Nerd Mission Control. Rows of desks with flat computer screens and keyboards, racks of machinery on the walls, cables carpeting the floor like a mass of snakes. Three guys and two girls who all looked like they popped out of the same pod as Zack, uniform in bad T-shirts and baggy jeans, sat among the screens, moving from desk to desk, tapping or mouse-clicking the occasional command.

"This," said Zack with pride, "is what I'm talking about."

"Looks like you could launch a space rocket from here."

"Ha!" Zack liked that. "Elon Musk only *wishes* he had a setup this sweet."

"Who?"

"The guy who sold PayPal to eBay for one point five billion. He used the money to create his own space-launch company."

"A guy from the Internet has his own space rockets now?"

"Yeah, welcome to the late twentieth century there, Mike."

"Funny. So if you're not launching the next probe to Mars in here . . ."

Zack sat down at one of the workstations, calling up a window with a sweep of its mouse, peering intently at the string of numbers it coughed up for him. "Do you even know why people want to go to Mars? I don't get it. There's nothing there except probably some bacteria, if we go up to look at the bacteria then the bacteria we carry will kill it and therefore we've made life on Mars extinct, we can't learn shit from the geology because the gravity isn't the same and gravity commands geology and—"

"Zack."

"—yeah. I know. I do that sometimes. No. Not sending a probe to Mars. Though if I did it would *rock* and would almost certainly drop a base on the moon on its way.

But no. What I'm doing in here is changing the nature of democracy. Did you ever read science fiction novels?"

"Not really."

He gave me a sour look out of the corner of his eye. "No kidding. Well, see, this seriously cool guy called Alfred Bester wrote a novel in the 1950s and I'm not going to get into it way deep except for there's this bit at the end where the guy in the novel has gotten hold of this stuff called PyrE, which I guess could be pronounced pyr-ee because the *e* is like a capital letter? And this stuff is thermonuclear explosive that can be detonated by thought alone. Like you could stash it someplace and then just *think* at it and it'd go off. And what he does is, instead of keeping it for himself, he scatters it among the people of the world. Which is an awesome thing. Because not only does it put the ability to fight power in ultimate weapon-of-mass-destruction mutually-assured-destruction kinda terms, but it also means that the ability to destroy the world is in the hands of people rather than governments. You got a cell phone?"

"Yeah."

"Is it the kind with the camera in?"

"Yeah."

"Take it out."

I fished my phone out of my pocket and showed it to him. Zack pointed at it. "PyrE."

"No no no. Phone. Fff oh nnnn."

He laughed and snatched it out of my hand. "Don't be giving me that shit. You're like a century out of date. You're a technological Neanderthal. You make fire with sticks. And fuck chimps out on the savannah. Or maybe dinosaurs."

My gag reflex convulsed.

Zack pulled out his own phone, something small and freaky-looking, and began ambidextrously operating both devices at once. "See, what these things do is put the ability to fight power in the hands of the people. And what denotes power, right now?"

"WMDs? Terrorist strikes? Shock and awe?"

"Old thinking, my brother. What's the one thing Osama bin Laden does that touches everyone on the planet?"

"Kills three thousand people in my fucking city?"

"Dude. He makes a video. He's made more videos than he's committed acts of terrorism. He controls the message, he controls the media outlets who fall all over themselves to give airtime to fucking Satan, and he controls the Western governments who blow days and weeks on hunting through the runtime for hidden messages to decode and clues to decipher. When all he's really doing is getting people to listen to what he's saying. Some old shitbag in a cave with a camera, man. *That's* the power. Getting the footage and getting it out."

Down the goddamn rabbithole again. I pulled up a chair. "Can I smoke in here, Zack?"

"Sure you can. Have one of mine, in fact. Robbie? Robbie! Can you gank us an ashtray from the other room?"

One of Zack's sticky-armpitted clones spoke in a wheedling tone that probably got him slapped around a lot in school. "We don't got any ashtrays in the other room."

"Jesus Christ, Robbie, I got a guest here. I need an ashtray."

"Got pizza boxes."

"Do any of the boxes still have pizza in them?"

"I think maybe Natalie didn't have the last slice of three-cheese."

"So that's our ashtray. Go get it. I'm really sorry about this, Mike. These people here are total fucking geniuses, but social skills? Forget it. Where was I?"

"Zack, I have no clue. Something about Osama bin Laden and cameras."

"Yes. Dude. It's all there." He passed me a cigarette, I tossed him the lighter. "The guy with the camera and the proximity to extraordinary information and the access to the media—that guy wins."

He tossed me the lighter back, and I thought a moment as I lit up. "So this is about cell phones with cameras."

"Right. People with the proximity to extraordinary information—that's anybody who happens to share a location with a sudden event, right? It used to happen with camcorders, people taping cops beating guys up for no reason other than that it got them off. But the thing about camcorders is that it's pretty easy to see you're using them." He held up his cell phone. "What am I doing right now? Am I reading a text message? An instant message? Trying to dial a number? Taking a photo of you? Shooting a video?" He angled the phone down. "Holding it like this, I'm not shooting a video. But I could be recording audio. And these phones are every-where, Mike. They're in *Iraq*."

"Soldiers in Iraq have cell phones?" Robbie put half a pizza box on the desk Zack was at, and Zack tipped ash on the rotting slice of pizza in there, which had to be at least a week old.

"Yeah." Zack giggled. He liked this bit. "In fact, there was a bit of a scandal. U.S. troops were racking up insane phone bills calling home. There were charity initiatives to get prepaid cell phones to troops. So I created phones-forourboys.org. I'm paying for a lot of their phones. And every soldier in Iraq who turns on a cell phone? They get a text message from me. A text and a configurator, which is a program sent over the air to their phone that installs itself. Now, for one thing, you've got to love the idea that porn is buying cell phones for soldiers, right? But that's not the bit that makes me fucking Einstein. The configurator is the bit that makes me fucking Einstein. Because it ties the phone to my system."

I just smoked and waited, as he grinned. I didn't need to prod him to keep talking. He was too into it, and I got the strong impression he didn't meet too many new people, especially not people prepared to listen to him talk.

"Okay, okay, I'll tell you." He laughed. "If you take a picture or shoot some video on a cell phone, it gives you the option to send it to someone, right? On a phone I've configured, it gives you an extra option: send it to me. Send it to me, and it goes to one of the servers, the big computers, that I keep in other countries. Because I don't need that shit on a computer in the U.S., you know? The content goes to me, and then my program sanitizes your phone. Deletes the content, the log of you sending it, everything. Did you catch the news this morning?"

"Five minutes in the airport at Vegas. Something about another clusterfuck in Iraq."

"Lousy video quality, right?"

"Right. Yes. No. Hold on. You're saying . . ."

"Yeah."

"That was you? You got that footage out?"

"Yeah. Some grunt on the ground didn't like the way

things were going that day and grabbed thirty seconds on his phone. And sent it to me. Not that he knew it was me, of course. No names, no pack drill. Fronts and cover companies, like a CIA operation, dude. Heh."

Zack jabbed out his cigarette in the pizza. There was a smell like plastic cooking over an uncleaned toilet. "You want a beer? Robbie, get us a couple of beers. Get beers for everybody. The cooler's full, right? So I co-locate this stuff all over the world. So when the Russian cops come for the front company in Moscow, the pictures of Mafiya paying off Duma members that have been captured by ordinary people on the street aren't on the servers in Moscow, you with me? They're in Tuvalu or South Africa or some fucking place. And this here"—Zack gestured broadly at his Mission Control—"this tells me where all my information is, all over the world. Cell phones and Internet-connected computers, dude. It's incredibly fucking simple. A support system for citizen journalism. News with no filters. And when we get something good, out it goes into the world. PyrE, see? I've given people all over the world the ability to fight power."

Beer came. I hoisted my cold dewed bottle to Zack Pickles, mad scientist and the first genuinely decent guy I'd met in what seemed like forever.

Chapter 46

The clock ticked around a couple of hours, and I figured it was time to call it a day. Or at least lunch. My mood was much improved. I had no idea how to get back to the place, but, with the little information I had, Zack did some Internet wizardry and got a printer to spit out a map with X marking the spot. He gave me back my phone—"my email, phone number, a few other bits, gimme a call, this was fun"—and had Robbie drive me back to the house.

There was a big, black, shiny car in the driveway. The door was unlocked. As I pushed it open, I heard the unmistakable sound of Trix having an orgasm.

And, a few seconds later, the new sound of a complete stranger, quite definitely male, having his own orgasm.

Chapter 47

I decided to stay outside for a little while, and have a cigarette and concentrate hard on not killing anyone. I think I finished the first one in two minutes, just dragging the life out of it, the last minute of which I spent watching a black limousine creeping down the street toward me. As it pulled up outside the house, I dug my hands into my pockets and waited. The sleek dark curve of the car opened up like a boiled mussel, and the chief of staff slid out, blinking in the sun.

"California's not fit for humans," he said, squinting at the bright sky. "Whole goddamn state should be sawed off the mainland and floated out into the Pacific. We'll get to that, mark my words. Except for Disneyland. I like Disneyland. We'll keep Disneyland. Staple it onto the end of Arizona or something. I always thought Disneyland should be its own state. Disneyland, the fifty-first state of America. Has a ring to it. California? Point the whole state toward Japan and kick it in the ass, that's what I say."

I felt like needling the old bastard. "What, the state that gave Ronald Reagan to politics?"

"Ronnie Reagan was no goddamned good to anyone," he snapped, surprising me. "Everyone knew he had Alzheimer's while he was president. He was only ever useful as a patsy. 'Ever met Ollie North, Mr. President?' 'I have no recollection of that because my brain is turning into a pile of scabs, Your Honor.' All he was ever good for. Everybody knows. Those episodes of *The West Wing* where the president has multiple sclerosis brainfarts? What do you think he was alluding to?"

I laughed. "So you did watch that show."

He found a pair of black shades in his jacket and fumbled them on. "CIA's been running Aaron Sorkin for years. He leaks this stuff out under cover of fiction to test the waters. Every time he gets too cute we plant crack on him in airports. Or make him write *Studio 60.*"

"You're full of shit."

He gave that creepy split-skull grin. "Want to know how much we paid Jim Nabors to shoot Reagan with a sniper rifle? Nothing. It was all done for the love of Rock Hudson."

"Can you do anything but lie? I mean, seriously?"

"I'm a politician, boy. I haven't told the truth since I was seven."

"What did you do when you were seven?"

"Chopped down a cherry tree. She betrayed you, didn't she?"

"What?"

"The girl. She's in there with some lawyer pounding her like he's drilling for oil off the California coast, right now. I bet he's already bust a nut once and is still digging away to prove what an incredibly California buffed-and-tanned physical specimen he is."

"What the hell has that got to do with you?"

"I warned you. I told you about her. I said she would betray you. You cannot trust women."

"I can't trust you."

"No. No, you can't. That's very good, Michael. But you can trust money. Money cannot lie. It is a means. It is a tool. And a bad workman cannot blame his tool. What have you done with the tools I gave you, Michael?"

I didn't say anything. He clacked his teeth together.

"You saved her life. That was good work. I bet she told you she loved you, after that. I bet she did. I bet she said nice things. But she lied, didn't she?"

"I don't think so. She just doesn't see it the same way. The, you know, the words. It means something a little different to her, that's all."

"We're in America, Michael. Telling someone you love them means only one thing, doesn't it? That you're not going to make the beast with two backs with the next warm body that falls in front of you. That's the American way. Or is that what you want? An America where love means nothing?"

"Are those the choices?"

"Hell, yes, those are the choices. How many do you want? We are fighting many wars, Michael, on many fronts. And this is the war at home. The war of meanings. The war of cultures. And right here, right now, you're on the line, Michael. I may be a professional politician with opiate lesions all over the front of my brain, but my money doesn't lie. She may be a sweet girl who's nice to you, but she's upstairs right now making a lawyer fill her with his little suits. Taking my side means only that honest American love will win the day."

"With this book? This thing, this reset button of yours?"

The shades made his eyes look like empty sockets. "A return to our roots. The mission would be easier if the book's effects transmitted over TV or the Net, but it naturally leads us to a grass-roots politics from the times of Washington and Lincoln. Town hall meetings. Stadiums. We can devise a million different events where the book is brought into play in front of crowds from all cultural and subcultural areas. We've been breeding pop stars in L.A. for exactly this kind of thing. Take some piece of greedy cracker trash with symmetrical features, vacuum the Cheetos dust off it, train it in a Disney pod, stick boobs on it and have its videos made by porn directors, and everyone under sixteen is yours. Also, the gay people. I never understood that. You could retrain fifty thousand of them at a time, putting the book in front of them at a stadium concert. Instill proper morals in them. Erase the sicknesses in their heads and make of them proper Americans who know what love means."

I looked at him. I had no idea what I was seeing. "You think this comes down to the nature of love in our time? Is that what you're selling?"

"I dunno. Are you buying it?"

"You are an evil old bastard."

"I am the chief of staff. You know how H.R. Haldeman described the job when he was chief of staff to Nixon? 'I'm the president's son of a bitch.'"

"Fuck me, I think you said something honest just then. I feel faint."

"These are hard times. I'm not going to be a child about the hard decisions. We're fighting what must be World War Six outside the country, and what is very probably Civil War Three within the country. You're going to help us bring that one to a conclusion. You'll save lives, I think. You'll certainly be saving a country and a way of life. Buck up, Michael. You're close to the end now. I can feel it in my bones. It'll all be over soon. And just in time, eh? You've got no money left, you're adrift in a state that should be hacked off the end of the continent like a tumor, and your girlfriend's upstairs fornicating with a *lawyer*. If that was my girl, well, I'd rather she were fucking a dog, wouldn't you? Or a donkey. I've seen those shows, down in Tijuana. Horrifying, really. Yet strangely hypnotic."

"Does it bother you at all that you make people's flesh crawl off their bones just by speaking out loud?"

"I run your country, son. It is only right and proper that the ordinary people should experience religious fear in my presence. I am the closest thing to God most folk will ever meet. And you, Michael: you are my personal Jesus. You are my intellectual child and the savior of that which I have created. I'm proud of you, boy. It's been a terrible journey for you, from your Manhattan Galilee to this, your California Calvary. But it's almost over now. I can feel it in my bone marrow."

"I think I'm going to be sick."

"Well, don't do it near me," he spat, scuttling backward. "These are new shoes. It's time for me to go. Go inside, now, Michael. Go and see your freak queen and her cockmonkey. Give 'em hell, boy. It's time to finish the job."

Chapter 48

I sat down in the guy's football field of a living room, put on the TV, turned it up good and loud, and waited. I wasted five minutes fiddling with my handheld and my cell phone, copying over Zack's email address to the computer and poking around in the logs and settings for a little bit.

"Hello. I'm Brom," came a voice from behind me.

He was taller than me, with the soft features, heavy brow, and thick hair of an eighties male model. The white T-shirt and black jogging pants were crisp enough to have been sold to him an hour earlier. I got up and we shook hands like men.

"Trix will be down in just a second," he said, searching my eyes for a reaction.

"Whatever." I smiled. "I don't keep my employees on a clock. Do you have time to talk for a few minutes?"

He waved me to the sofa and took the big, high-backed armchair for himself. I suppressed a smile. Sitting down, I asked him if Trix had told him anything about the case.

He wriggled a bit. "We haven't had a chance to talk properly beyond, you know, catching up and stuff."

I let that hang just a little too long, to see him wriggle a bit more. "Well, okay. I've been hired by an individual in Washington, D.C., to track down a stolen item. The trail's led me here, to a law firm in Los Angeles. I was wondering if you could tell me anything about the firm in question."

This worked better for him. I needed something from him. Anyone could see from the way his posture shifted that he liked it when people needed something from him. I decided that I could get to hate this guy pretty quickly.

"Shoot," Brom said. "Anything I can do, really."

"For a friend of Trix?"

"Right." He coughed.

"Islip, Sinclair, and Collis. Ring any bells?"

He stiffened. "There's no way in hell Frank Islip is trafficking in stolen goods."

"Not saying it's him, or any of the partners. But someone is at the very least using the firm's identity in connection with this item."

"Islip, Sinclair is an incredibly important player in the L.A. legal community. No one—"

"I'm betting that no one in Las Vegas has even heard of them."

Brom smiled and relaxed. "—ah. Yes, well, that'd make sense."

"Could you possibly get me an introduction? I realize it's imposing."

"Well, yes, it is, a bit."

"But, then again, you have just fucked my assistant. And I'll be leaving her here once I'm done with interviewing at that firm, so you two can catch up at your leisure."

"Mike?" Trix had come down the stairs.

"Hi, Trix. Just tying up the loose ends here. So could you get me an introduction? The sooner the better, obviously."

Brom didn't speak. The silence turned venomous. Trix came and sat next to me. I moved over a space and watched Brom.

Eventually, he said, slowly, "I'm actually attending a private party at their offices tonight. I'll speak to someone there and get you in tomorrow morning. You can stay here tonight, obviously."

"Thank you, Brom. Much obliged."

He stood, a sharp movement. "My ticket's a plus-one,

Trix. I'd love it if you came with me. No dress code. Now, if you'll excuse me, I brought some work home with me. Make yourselves at home, and I'll be back in a few hours."

He padded quickly out of the living room.

"That was a prickish thing to do, Mike," Trix hissed.

"So?"

"What do you mean, so? What's wrong with you? No, forget I said that. I know exactly what's wrong with you."

"No shit, Sherlock."

She tried a smile. "I thought you were Sherlock and I was Watson."

I couldn't hold it in anymore. "You *fucked* him?"

"Goddamnit, Mike, we talked about this. He's an old friend. An old lover, okay? He's a very sweet man and he's good in bed and we haven't seen each other in years and it felt really nice *especially* after having had a fight with you and we didn't hurt anybody except maybe some willfully dumb guy who refuses to listen to a word I say. And I don't think it even hurt you, not really. It *offended* you. You think because we sleep together you own my sexuality, and you really don't."

I didn't have an answer to that, but it didn't seem to slow Trix down.

"You know what the worst thing is? I told you I love you—"

"You never said any such goddamn thing."

241

"—told you I *could* love you and you went white as a sheet and stiff as a goddamn board. And not in the good way. You act like you own a piece of me and you don't even love me. You like being the white knight and you like, excuse my arrogance but fuckit I know who I am, a hot girl taking pleasure from you, but you won't let a damn thing get under your skin or disturb the shallowness you cultivate to get through the fucking day, Mike."

"Shallowness. This is going back to the goddamn book, isn't it?"

She laughed without mirth. "I guess you're hellbent on getting that thing and handing it over now. Get the likes of me reprogrammed. I'm gonna look hot in an apron, barefoot in the kitchen, right?"

"You can hide out here with Brom. I won't tell."

"You know? I might. He's at least aware of the world outside and trying to change it for the better. I don't know what you're doing anymore, Mike. This isn't fun anymore."

"Guess what. Not everything is fun. We deal anyway." My cell phone went off. "Excuse me."

I walked out of the living room, put the front door on the latch, and sat down on the porch outside.

"It's Zack. The creepiest thing just happened, dude."

"What?"

"Two isweartogod Men in Black just left, with an old guy in tow. They asked me about you."

"Oh, Jesus."

"What was that about? It wasn't a raid. Hell, the old guy asked if we did any medical-fetish porno and I gave him a DVD."

"That, Zack, was my client."

"Damn, Mike. I've met some weird people in this town, politicians and lawyers, but I never had anything like this."

"Yeah, I'm sorry. I have no idea how that happened. If it helps, they're in no position to drop the boom on you. You're cool."

"If you say so, dude. But *damn* that was weird."

"Listen . . . You've dealt with lawyers?"

"Oh, they're the worst. I have to chase them out of here with a broom. Sick stuff, lemme tell ya."

"Do you know an outfit called Islip Sinclair Collis?"

"What the fuck are you into, Mike?"

"Zack, please."

"I won't deal with 'em. Life's too short. And those parties of theirs, Jesus."

I pulled a cigarette. "Tell me about the parties, Zack."

"First I'm going to send a configurator to your phone. You carrying any other Internet-enabled devices I should know about?"

Chapter 49

I walked quickly through the living room into the kitchen. Opened the drawer I wanted, threw out the false bottom, and took out the Ruger. Loaded it, slowly. Walked back into the living room with the Ruger heavy in my right hand. Grabbed Trix's hand with my left, yanking her up off the sofa.

"Where's Brom working?"

"What?"

"*Now,* Trix."

I dragged her into the hallway, where we heard the clicking of a keyboard. There was an expansive home office at the back of the house. Brom was working at a big black desktop computer on a big black desk. He spoke without looking around. "Anything you need?"

I hit him in the back of the head with the butt of the Ruger. He slid off the chair like a sack of hammers.

Trix punched me in the shoulder with her free hand. "What the hell? Mike!"

I looked at her. She got scared in a way I didn't like. But I didn't have time for anything else.

"Get up," I said to Brom. Blood was trickling out of his hair onto the back of the T-shirt.

"Christ," he groaned. "I'm sorry I had sex with her, all right? I'm sorry. Fucking lunatic."

"Trix, you need to tell me you had protected sex with this man."

"Of course I did. Mike, we can talk about this. Don't, don't do whatever's in your mind. We can fix this."

"Brom, you need to tell Trix all about this party at Islip tonight."

He twisted around on the ground to face me. "Fuck you."

I stamped on his balls. As he convulsed forward, I kicked his head to the ground and put my foot on the side of it. Going down on one knee, I pressed the Ruger to his temple and pulled the hammer back.

"I don't particularly like having turned into all the assholes I've been dealing with since I started this case, Brom. But you've done it to me. All of you. All of you monsters. So now I'm like you. Now either you can tell her what these parties are, or I can put a bullet through your brain, have the White House chief of staff sanitize your murder and this location so it becomes like you never even existed, and then tell her myself. Tell me what happens next, Brom. Tell me if I'm killing you."

"They're sex parties."

"What kind of sex parties, Brom?"

"Sex parties with . . . with teenagers."

I screwed the muzzle of the gun into his temple until the skin broke. "Stop fucking with me."

"With kids. Okay? With virgin kids. Kids who don't have HIV."

"Yeah," I said, mostly to myself. "Falconer. That god-damn Falconer was right. Who'd've thought it?"

I felt Trix go cold in my hand. "Brom. What are you talking about?"

"The upper ranks of power in this town . . . You try getting laid in this town without having a current HIV test. You can't. Sex parties, forget it. Once you've been around a while, herpes is the best you can hope for. If you like group sex, unprotected sex, hurting people . . . Look, it's something I have to be part of, okay? If I want the power in this town to be able to change anything, I have to be part of the system."

"They call them roulette parties, Trix," I said quietly. "They get two or three pretty kids, drug them to their eye-balls, and then everyone at the party screws them. And then they place bets on which of the kids will end up HIV positive. That's why I needed to know if you had protected sex. Because I doubt that this is the first invite Brom's gotten."

"I've only been to three! Three!" Brom shrieked.

"Now, Brom. My life is a mess of shitty coincidences. So you tell me now: Is there anything special about tonight's party? I didn't like your reaction when you told me Frank Islip would never traffic in stolen goods. Because I didn't give you a name. I gave you the firm's title. And when I gave you an out, you took it so fast I couldn't see your ass for dust."

"They bought something. An antique. Something that'll give the community political leverage in Washington. I don't know what it is. They're showing it off tonight."

"And we know what that is, don't we, Trix?"

I let go of her hand. She didn't move away.

"Yeah. We do. Your ticket's plus-one, Brom?"

Brom didn't answer.

Trix's hand reached for my gun. Our eyes met. I slipped the gun into her hand.

She moved the gun muzzle around his face, and slowly pushed it into his eye.

She ground out the words. "Plus-one?"

". . . yes."

"Well, I'd love to come to the party with you, Brom. But we need to figure out a way for Mike to get in, too."

Chapter 50

I drew the living room curtains, put my foot through the phone in the room, and unplugged it from the wall just to make damn sure. Trix found some fur-lined handcuffs in his bedroom, which I decided not to think about, and we put a dining room chair in the living room, sat Brom down in it, and cuffed him to it.

I sat in his armchair and looked at the big Ruger Super Blackhawk in my hand. "This thing's going to be a problem," I said.

"Are you going to take it?" Trix said. She didn't like looking at it. She'd handed it back to me like it was a dead rat once we'd gotten off Brom in his office, and washed her hands in the kitchen sink afterward, looking a little nauseous.

"It makes too damn much noise. These things go off

like God punching the world. Did you never see Dirty Harry? Everyone else's guns go bang bang, and his gun goes *pow*. I fire this in an office building and everyone's going to see the windows rattle."

"Are you expecting to have to use it, is what I'm saying, Mike."

"Yeah. Yeah, I am. I'm not going to be able to bluff my way into the building. They know Brom, he said he's been there before. What's the parking situation there, Brom?"

Brom had pretty much given up, and sagged there like jelly. "Underground car park. Security at the elevator, security at the thirty-third floor. Where the party is."

"Okay," I said. "Not as bad as I expected. I'm just wondering where they'll be keeping the book."

"Frank Islip's office. His personal safe. I've seen it. He keeps his good stuff there. Likes to show people things."

"Why are you being so helpful all of a sudden?"

"Because I'm not the bad guy here." He looked at Trix. "I'm not a bad guy. I do what I have to in order to remain in a position to help people."

"Bullshit."

Brom prickled. "Do you know why I became a lawyer? Do you? Because I wanted a say in the shape of society. If I have to join the Pirates—"

"The what?"

"That's what they call themselves. The Pirates of the Pacific. A bunch of them were in Skull and Bones at Yale—"

"Oh my God," yelped Trix. "I've heard of them. I think three or four presidents have been in Skull and Bones. All kinds of weird political conspiracy stuff, you know?" She turned to me. "Skull and Bones was implicated in the opium trade, and they're considered racist and proslavery, Mike. A bunch of Yale's residential colleges are named after slave owners. We're gonna walk into this party and find three or four pretty black kids waiting to get raped."

"Yeah," I said. "Why are you suddenly being cooperative, Brom?"

"If you do something to disempower the Pirates," said Brom, "then by default the younger generation, like me, gains more power in town. I'll give you all the help you need."

I smiled at Brom. "You fucking maggot."

"Hold on," said Trix. "Give me a second here."

She looked at Brom. He withered a little under her intent gaze. And then she looked across at me.

"Why aren't we just calling the cops, Mike? I mean, yes, I know, powerful people, political clout, friends in high places, I get all that. But why aren't we just feeding Brom to the cops and letting them get the story out of him?"

Brom cleared his throat. "These people run L.A.'s legal—"

"I said I get that, Brom. I'm saying that even the cops can't ignore a confession from a legal player like you. Why don't we feed him to the cops, Mike?"

I pulled out another cigarette. I'd been using an expensive-looking modern-art sculpture thing as an ashtray. "Can't do it, Trix."

"Because of what Brom says?"

"Because we'd lose the book. We can call the cops once we're in there. We do it now and that book'll disappear into some secure location we'll never find. And I want this ended."

"Mike, that's really dangerous. And I don't mean for us. They're going to have sex on kids. If we get there late, if we can't get to a phone, if the cops don't listen . . . something awful's going to happen to them."

"I know. The only thing in our favor is that they're not going to be expecting anyone to break into a very secret, very private party. There'll be security, but it won't be heavy, because heavy security draws attention of its own. And the last thing they want is attention."

"Mike, I don't think the book matters anymore."

"It does. It does to me. I want out of this, and the book

gets me out. I'm starting to look back with nostalgia at the middle-aged ostrich fuckers, Trix. Help me out with this and you never have to see me again."

"What makes you think I never want to see you again?"

"Giving me shit about the case and sleeping with the white slaver here were clues. I'm a detective."

"Mike . . ." Trix sighed and leaned over in her chair until her head was touching her legs. "Mike, I told you and told you. This is how I choose to live. It doesn't affect us at all."

"It affects me. And you already think I'm a monster for wanting to hand over the book."

She studied me, tiredly. "I don't care anymore. I just want to be done with this. You're exhausting me. This is exhausting me."

"Yeah." I flicked ash onto the rich carpet, quite deliberately. "Now, Brom. I'm going to uncuff you, and you're going to draw me a little map of the offices we're attending. And then you're going to tell me how the entrance procedure works. Trix, you want to start getting ready. Time's ticking away."

Chapter 51

After some extended foraging through that stupidly huge house that probably took me into another time zone, I found Brom's liquor cabinet. A walk-in liquor cabinet. In there, cobwebby, was a whiskey that was old enough to be Trix's mother. I poured myself three fingers and sat down alone with Brom's map. It wasn't bad. Too detailed to be a complete fabrication. It was a new building, he'd said, barely two years old, and gave a pretty good description of the environs. Good enough for me to figure out a remarkably stupid stunt, anyway.

Two elevators served the offices. He'd marked the positions he'd noticed security agents in, the last two times he'd attended the place. The bullpen area was cleared as party space. Islip's office was fairly distant from it. There'd be a sequence of locked doors to defeat, of course, but one thing you're taught as an investigator is how to, well, commit crimes. I'd taken a couple of things from the kitchen that, with some judicious bending and twisting, would serve as tools for breaking and entering.

The last few days had either made me a better detective or a better criminal.

Getting to the elevators. Using the elevator without detection. Getting to Islip's office without detection. I wasn't overly worried about the safe. I knew where it was, and there's no such thing as an uncrackable safe. I was worried about getting out. If I had to hurt someone to get up there, I'd have less than fifteen minutes before the flags went up. And despite what I'd said to Trix, I knew that calling the cops wouldn't do a goddamn thing unless I got very creative.

The whiskey was shivering in the glass. My hand was shaking. I polished off the last of it and placed the glass upside down on the nearest table.

Chapter 52

The ride into Beverly Hills was dark and hot. The black handheld in my jacket pocket jabbed into my chest for most of the way there. I cradled the unloaded Ruger in my hands, thinking furiously. Running every possible move and outcome in my head. My heart was hammering, and my nerves jangled with stress. I found myself grinding my teeth, and forced myself still. I wanted a cigarette. I wanted a cigarette and, stupidly, pemmican. I read all the James Bond books as a kid, and, in one of them, Bond prepares for an infiltration by holing up someplace until night, smoking cigarettes, and eating wedges of pemmican. I wanted cigarettes and pemmican and to be James Bond. Instead, I was sweating myself to death in the trunk of a lawyer's car en route to Beverly Hills.

Brom finally popped the trunk. I sat up sharply. We were in an underground carport, dark and cool. Like a good boy, Brom had parked far away from the elevators, several whitewashed concrete stanchions obscuring us from whoever might be over there.

I pulled the ammunition from my jacket pocket and began to reload the Ruger. "How many?" I whispered.

"Just one, by the elevator. There's a restroom around the corner from that."

"Good. Brom, when all hell breaks loose, and it will— you grab Trix and you get the hell out of there. That's all you have to do. Is that clear?"

Cogs worked in Brom's brain. "You're going to let me get away?"

"Get Trix out of there and no one needs to know you were ever involved. And I'm sorry about the crack on the head and all, but I was kind of pissed."

Brom stuck out his hand. "So we're even?"

My face must've changed significantly, because he instantly went pale. "No, Brom, we're not even. I am simply choosing not to care about you. And if you don't get Trix somewhere safe, you don't get to live until the end of the week. Are we clear on that?"

He stuck his hand in his pocket.

I clambered out of the car. Trix waited beside it, very quiet.

"Just stick to the sidelines," I said to her, "and get the fuck out of Dodge when it all goes off. I'll get your money to you in a couple of days."

"I don't want the money," she said.

"So what do you want?"

She didn't say anything.

I looked around. It was just us in the carport.

"Okay," I said. "Let's do something really goddamn stupid."

Chapter 53

I moved around the carport, taking cover where I could, as Trix and Brom walked directly to the elevators—two of them, side by side, with an alcove beside the far one—talking loudly, as I'd asked. The uniformed security agent wasn't young, but looked beefy. He was deferential to Brom and Trix, which was good. There are two kinds of security—the kind who thinks he works for the security firm, and the kind who thinks he works for the firm's clients. The first kind are tough and alert, because they work for the reputation of the firm. The second kind concentrates on appearance to keep the client pleased. This guy was definitely the second kind, which meant I had a chance.

I listened to his voice as he spoke to Brom and Trix, marking him and his plus-one off on his clipboard. Phlegmy, slow. He thumbed the radio on his shoulder, letting security upstairs know the pair were coming up. He walked them to the elevator, saw them into it, and turned around.

As the doors were closing, Brom and Trix must've seen me jab my thumb and forefinger into the security guy's throat from behind, and then drive the butt of the gun into the back of his head. He almost shrugged off the first blow, gagging as I killed his voice. The fourth took him down.

I almost popped a rib dragging the bastard around the corner into the toilets. I gagged him with a wad of toilet paper and his own tie and cuffed him around the toilet before locking the stall from the inside. Coughing some spit down into my throat, I reached around and thumbed his radio.

"Need the john. Ate something bad. Clipboard's by the elevators—come down and cover me for ten minutes. Gonna sign off, this hurts like hell." I switched the radio off before anyone could answer, and climbed out of the top of the stall with the clipboard.

Outside, I propped the clipboard on the corner, so whoever came down had to turn their back on the elevator and walk away from it to retrieve it. I dashed to the alcove and waited.

Two minutes crept by. Just as I was sure I'd fucked it up, the elevator pinged, and a skinny security man came down. He looked around for the clipboard. Spotted it. Walked toward it. I very silently moved to the elevator. He bent down to pick the clipboard up. I reached a hand inside and above the elevator door. Found what I hoped for, and smacked it to the right with my finger. Slid in and punched the door-close button, pressed against the left side of the elevator.

Above the door was a security camera that trained down on the inside of the elevator car. Smacking it to the right meant that it could only see the right half of the car. I stayed on the left, where the control panel was, and punched in 32.

There was blood on the butt of the Ruger. I rubbed it off on my pants leg. And then looked down. Suddenly I'd become cavalier about blood. I did not enjoy this about myself. Taking a deep breath, I tried to remember who I was before this whole thing started. I came back to myself, a little bit.

The elevator pinged at 32. I stepped out carefully into darkness. The rest of the building was, of course, empty.

Brom's map was in my head. I was below everything he'd detailed for me, and I looked up, measuring the relative position of everything above me.

It was a new building. And Brom's powers of description had given me the idea. New office buildings tend to prize flexibility. So what they do is build the framework and hang the walls from the framework, using adhesive wainscot to fix them to the floor. It allows the owners to change the structure of their office design. There have been stories of people in high-risk jobs coming to work in the morning to discover that their little office is entirely missing—workmen have come in the night to take out the walls and change the workplace design.

Plasterboard and plastic. Paneled ceilings. Stuff that breaks and cuts.

I broke a couple of locks and moved around until I found some desks and chairs. The clock was running in my head. My unconscious guy with the phantom shits would be given ten minutes, if I was lucky. And if the bastard didn't wake up first. I didn't have a lot of time, and past history made it disgustingly clear that I had no luck at all. Working as quietly as I could without wasting time, I stacked chairs up on a desk for a makeshift ladder, and got under the ceiling. It was a gridwork of metal strips with plastic panels. The panels were just laid on. I pushed one up. There was a space, maybe a couple of feet, between this ceiling and the underside of the next floor up. Trunks of wires ran here and there. The dust would've choked a regiment. I prayed to anything that might be paying attention that the metal frame held my weight, and lifted myself up.

I spidered myself over the plastic panels, keeping

hands, knees, and feet on the metal struts. Everything creaked and groaned a little, but held. Good. I moved along the space like the world's most retarded crab, trying to keep the map straight in my head. Eventually, I picked my spot, and turned myself around so my back was supported by the metal. From my jacket, I took the sharpest knife I could find in Brom's kitchen. It had taken a good thirty minutes, late in the afternoon, picking through all his shiny, pricey kitchen equipment, most of which had never been used. He only bought the best stuff, beautiful selections of samurai-quality hand-made carbon-blade cutting tools. I'd taken this one to a fine edge on a ceramic whetstone he'd left out on display without ever touching, and tested it on various of his possessions. There was even a half-inch gully in his marble countertop.

I put it into the underside of the floor. It did not exactly cut like butter. I wriggled under the pommel of the blade and put both hands into it, pushing upward, terrified the extra force would put me back through the ceiling and on to the floor.

The blade punched through. I started sawing, as fast as I dared. This stunt was both clever and staggeringly stupid. There were fair odds that someone was up there watching the end of the knife bobbing up and down like the fin of a drunken shark.

Within a couple of minutes—and, at that point, it was two minutes too long—I'd sawed a flap in the upstairs floor. Scoring a diagonal between the end of both cuts, I squirmed back to the corner and pushed. It was stiff. Without the scoreline, it would have groaned. But it folded along the score, and cracked. Audibly cracked. I grabbed the edge of the floor, cutting my palm, and pulled myself up in panic.

No one there. Music leaked in from beyond the closed east door of Islip's outer office. The west door led to his inner office. The music must've masked the sound of the flooring cracking. I almost cried at the thought that I'd finally had a bit of luck.

Pulling myself out of the crawlspace felt like dragging myself free of quicksand. I went straight to the west door and checked it for alarms. It was clean. I pulled out the other things I'd lifted from Brom's house and quickly jimmied the old-fashioned lock on the door. It clicked open.

Islip's office looked like an old English drawing room, with silky wallpaper, ornate gilt-framed oil paintings of military men on horseback, and antique high-backed armchairs. On the wall behind the desk was a big oil portrait of a pirate with a beard you could lose a dog in pouring boiling oil on what I presumed were seagoing taxmen. I lifted it off the wall to reveal the safe.

And, of course, it was the picture that was alarmed.

Chapter 54

I invented five new swearwords in six seconds.

Dashing to the door, I jabbed the jimmy into the lock, immobilizing it. A chair went under the door handle. I ran back to the safe. It was electronic. Brom had told me it was an old-style dial-tumbler design. I went down and peered at the numeric keypad at an angle. The most-used keys pick up more dirt than the others. But this damn thing was new. In my pocket, I had some talc lifted from Brom's kitchen that I'd wrapped in a square of kitchen paper. I unwrapped it and blew a little over the keypad, and then blew lightly at the keypad itself. One, five, six, and eight looked like they'd attracted more powder than the others, which meant they were slightly stickier, which meant they'd been used more. I hoped.

Someone banged on the door.

I started tapping in variations on 1568. It took me five or six goes before I noticed the little LED display on the face of the safe.

ALARM-LOCK.

The damn thing immobilized when the alarm went off.

With the alarm still beeping away, the element of surprise had kind of faded away a while back.

So I took out the Ruger and shot the safe.

The *pow* was deafening in the enclosed space. The windows wobbled in their frames. The safe spat out a shower of sparks, the LED going dead. I'd put the big bullet right where I assumed the locking mechanism to be, and the door resentfully eased open by about an inch. I put Brom's kitchen knife in the gap and started levering with all the strength I had left.

There was a crunching, the blade snapped off, and the door came away. I pulled the door back as far as I could, and looked inside, heart in my mouth.

The book was in there.

It had to be the book. It was ancient. Big, with gray leather covers, mold greening the corners.

The banging on the door turned to thumping. Someone was throwing their body against it.

I took the book out gingerly, and laid it on the desk. The second it touched the surface, my head started swimming, like I'd taken a heavy toke off a strong joint. I shook it off and opened the book. The front cover touched the desk surface and it happened again. I felt my eyes widen and my head kind of lurch to attention, going light.

I took out my phone, found the number I wanted, and hit redial.

"It's McGill," I said. "I'm sure you know where I am. I have what you want. Send in the cavalry. And that's *now*, not in five minutes' time."

"We're outside," rasped the voice I'd learned to hate. "Three minutes, Mr. McGill."

Three minutes. Probably not enough time. But I had to try it.

I took out the handheld computer.

Chapter 55

Mr. McGill," came the voice. From the door.

I walked to it, gun in hand. "Are we all clear?"

"Of course. Open the door."

"Hold on," I said. I pulled the makeshift lockpicker out of the door, very quietly slid the chair away, and walked back to the desk. "Come on in."

The chief of staff entered with two men in black. He took two steps and stopped.

I had the Ruger pressed to the closed book.

"What exactly is transpiring here, Mr. McGill?"

"Insurance," I said, much more calmly than I expected. "Pick up the handheld device on the desk there."

"You can't possibly expect to shoot me before these people unload into your body, Mr. McGill." The two

Secret Service men had both drawn on me, rock steady and aimed at my eyes.

"I'm not aiming at you, sir. Look at me. I'm aimed at the book."

"What is this?"

"The book's not going to be a whole hell of a lot of use to you with five large holes in it. Pick up the handheld. I want to see my money transferred into my account before I hand the book over."

"This is stupid. I'm the White House chief of staff. I don't lie."

"There's no way your boys can take me out before I fire into the book. I've already taken first pressure. If I cough, bullets go through this book. Destroying words. Destroying whatever crap is really in the covers. It'll be useless to you. And after the week I've had, I really, really couldn't give a shit what happens next."

"We have your friend Trix, you know. Her lawyer friend bolted the second the alarm went off."

"She's not my friend. She's someone I was sleeping with until she slept with someone else."

He smiled his awful smile. "Yes, I'm aware of that. I did try to warn you."

I smiled back at him. "Yes, you did. Pick up the handheld."

"Yes," he said. "I will. A job well done, Mr. McGill, against astonishing odds."

He took the device, and his long fingers began playing its keyboard.

"Mike?" came a voice from outside.

"Bring her through," the chief of staff absently muttered, working the device. Trix, with a foul look on her face, emerged from the outer offce.

"So you're doing it," she said to me.

"You're damn right I am. And I don't care if you're disappointed."

"Meh. It's been a day of disappointments. It's not like you're surprising me with your spinelessness, Mike."

"Yeah, well. The one thing my life has taught me is that there's always space for surprise."

"An excellent lesson to end the day with, Mr. McGill." The chief smiled. He put the device on the desk and swiveled it around to show me the screen. "A completed, irrevocable transfer of funds, available immediately for your use. You have lived up to your peculiar reputation and my faith in you, Mr. McGill. Now, the book, if you please."

Watching the Secret Service men, I slowly laid the Ruger on the book and backed away.

"You can keep the gun, too." I smiled. "I'm done with it."

I walked around the table and picked up the hand-held. The chief walked around the other side and laid his hands on the book, reverently.

"I'm done," I said. "We're leaving."

"Yes, yes," he said, waving his hand. "You'll never see me again, Mr. McGill. Unless you attend one of our readings, of course. It may do you good. Return you to moral balance."

"I'm doing okay," I said, taking Trix's wrist. "Have fun."

I walked her out of the office, through the outer office, and into the bullpen. The Secret Service was every-where, encircling the great and the good of the party. In the middle of the room were three very scared Latino adolescents in white smocks. The men in black nodded us through, and I pulled Trix toward the elevators.

"Don't touch me," she said, as I punched the call button.

"Please, Trix. A couple more minutes and you can do what you like. Just work with me here."

Both elevators pinged, within a few seconds of each other.

"Please," I said to no one. "One more time. Just for us."

The first elevator to open was empty. I shoved Trix into it. A second later, the other elevator opened. And LAPD poured out of it. An absolute flood of ugly men in blue. I leapt in next to Trix and hit the button for the underground carport.

"What the hell was that?" Trix yelped.

"I called the cops."

"Mike!"

Chapter 56

What did you tell the cops to get them there so fast?"

"I told them someone armed was robbing Frank Islip's safe."

"Oh my God. And they're walking into—"

"Into a distinctly criminal sex party apparently attended by the White House chief of staff."

Trix just looked at me, mouth open and eyes wide. I knew I was grinning. I couldn't help it. I knew that if I could get through the last ten minutes, her reaction alone would make it all worth it. And, my God, it did. And I wasn't done yet.

"It's going to be interesting when the press arrive, don't you think?"

"You didn't. You couldn't. There's no way you could arrange that."

"See, I met a very interesting guy this morning. You'd like him, actually. Zack Pickles. He works in porno, but he does it to raise money for what he's really interested in. Which is moving a certain kind of information around. He called the press for me. But what gave me the really good idea was you."

"What did I do?"

"You uploaded photos from the handheld to your hosting site, didn't you? I poked around the handheld a bit, and saw how it worked. Email attachments. Like the photos my ex and her partner send to me. Just stick 'em to an email and off they go. That's what made me think of it."

"What did you do?"

The elevator pinged, and we got out. Of course, Brom was long gone, so we just walked up the exit ramp to the street outside.

"Well, I had to give the bastard the book. There was no way around that. But his big idea of doing the Freedom Train thing, getting people inside town halls and exposing them to the damn thing—and I tell you, that book is weird—it was only ever going to work if people didn't know what they were letting themselves in for. It's right there in the book, on the first page. Someone wrote instructions for use of the book. And the chief of staff obviously wasn't going to have people warned before-hand. That wasn't the plan."

We got to the street. I stopped, looked up at the night, and drew a long breath.

"Mike, if you don't tell me what you did and I mean *stat* I'm going to rip off your junk and—"

"I photographed the book with the handheld, Trix. The whole thing is only ten pages. I photographed every page and uploaded the photos to Zack Pickles's secure hosting site. Those photos are going to be all over the Internet in the next ten minutes. Because everyone's been telling me that the Internet and everything on it is the mainstream now."

Oh, yes, it was time for a cigarette. And this one was most definitely the Cigarette of Victory. I lit it and threw the rest of the pack down a drain.

"It's no good to the White House when everyone knows exactly what it is and exactly what it does. No one's going to go near it. Hell, the White House won't even bother taking it out. It becomes a curio, a weird antique, a discussion point for constitutional scholars and poli-sci majors. It's . . . defused. And I still got paid, and they can't pull the money back. We win. We beyond win. We are made of win. My God, it's full of win. And so on."

Trix threw her arms around me and kissed me, and I felt stress unpin the muscles in my back for the first time in a day.

"My God, it's full of win?"

"There's no way in hell you haven't seen *2001*, Trix, so don't even—"

"Yes." She smiled. "I've seen it. I just . . . I really didn't think you were going to do anything but hand the thing over and take the money."

"Yeah, I know. You know why you thought that? Because I decided to make it hard for you to trust me. Now, here's how it's going to be."

Her eyebrows went up. "Dear God. Is this your special Patriarchy voice?"

"Yes, it is, and you are just a girl, so you will be quiet and listen while I tell you how it's going to be. You know how hard it was for you to trust me today? That's how hard it is for me to trust you with the whole sex-fiend thing. But I am a man, and therefore capable of change and compromise. So here's the deal. You can sleep with any woman you want—"

Trix thumped me in the chest, laughing in disbelief. "You total pig bastard!"

"—let me finish. You can sleep with any woman you want. You can sleep with hairy-nippled women, you can sleep with skinhead women in combat boots who smoke unfiltered French cigarettes, you can sleep with women who inject their nether regions with warm salty water. And as for everything else . . ."

I stopped. I stroked her cheek.

". . . as for everything else. Just come home at night, would you? Do what you like, do what you have to. Just come home to me at night. Because I love you."

Chapter 57

Of course, the first apartment we took together turned out to have been vacated due to the owner, a dog breeder, having been beaten to death with the corpse of a chihuahua. And after the third break-in we realized that our repeat burglars were a team of necrophiles trying to retrieve some dead bodies they'd stored in the walls.

But we did okay.

Acknowledgments

I know I'm going to forget someone, because I'm writing this in the pub and the deadline for this page was four days ago. So, in the order they occur to me as I work through my third Red Bull:

Miss Wurzel Tod, the inimitable Suzanne Gerber of Basel, who was the first person to put the words *Godzilla* and *bukkake* together in the same sentence. Susannah Breslin, late of New Orleans, and the late Leticia Blake of Los Angeles, whose (the former) writings on and (the latter) experience of the sex trade informed many scenes. Dr. Joshua Ellis (no relation) of Las Vegas, who put one of the settings in my head.

Margo Eve of Virginia, the original Pervert Academic. Lydia Wills of Manhattan, my literary agent, who basically bugged the shit out of me until I wrote the first ten thousand words of this book to make her go away, and then pulled on me the worst trick of my life by selling it in two weeks. Any factual errors in this book should be blamed on her: not because they're her fault, but because it pleases me to do so. My media agent, Angela Cheng Caplan of Hollywood, for nagging me whenever Lydia paused for breath. Xeni Jardin of Los Angeles and William Gibson of Vancouver, for generally being help and inspiration.

And to my various hosts during my American tour of 2000, which gave me the framework for the book—New York, Columbus, San Antonio, Vegas, and L.A. (There was also a stop in San Francisco, but fiction will never top the Bay Area for outright surrealism.)

If there's anyone I've forgotten, please accept my apologies and thanks, and blame encroaching senility. Or Lydia.

Warren Ellis
Rainy Southeast England
March 2007